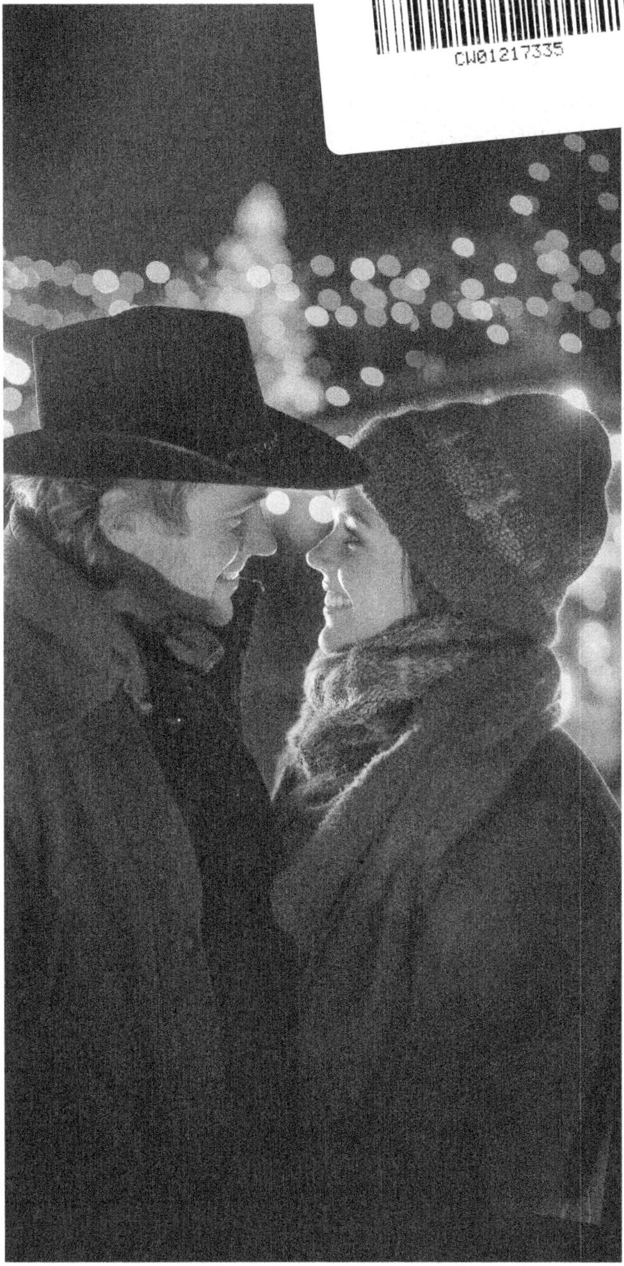

WRANGLING A CHRISTMAS COWBOY
Copyright © November 2024 by Katie Lane

All rights reserved. Except for use in any review, the reproduction or utilization of this work in whole or in part in any form by any electronic, mechanical or other means, now known or hereinafter invented, including xerography, photocopying and recording, or in any information storage or retrieval system, is forbidden without the written permission of the publisher.

This book is a work of fiction. Names, characters, places, and incidents are a product of the writer's imagination. All rights reserved. Scanning, uploading, and electronic sharing of this book without the permission of the author is unlawful piracy and theft. To obtain permission to excerpt portions of the text, please contact the author at *katie@katielanebooks.com*

Thank you for respecting this author's hard work and livelihood.

Cover Design and Interior Format
© KILLION GROUP INC.

Wrangling a CHRISTMAS COWBOY

HOLIDAY RANCH
SIX

KATIE LANE

*To my faithful readers
who love a good cowboy hero*

Chapter One

EVERYTHING HAPPENS FOR a reason.

Noelle Holiday firmly believed this. Call it fate or, as her grandma Mimi liked to say, divine intervention. As far as Noelle was concerned, there was no such thing as random luck.

So when Sheryl Ann called and asked Noelle if she could take over Nothin' But Muffins while she was in Big Springs handling some family issues—getting her brother out of jail and into rehab, as rumor had it—Noelle didn't hesitate to pack up her bags and head to her hometown of Wilder, Texas.

It wasn't like she had anything keeping her in Dallas. She'd graduated from culinary school and had yet to find a job. She'd broken up with her boyfriend and had no interesting prospects. And she could post to her almost four thousand social media followers from anywhere.

Which was exactly what she was getting ready to do.

With Nothin' But Muffins closed for the day and with Thanksgiving less than a week away,

Noelle had decided it would be a good time to do a pie post.

Pies were Noelle's specialty. Her mama made the best pies in the county and Noelle carried on the family tradition. One day, she would open up her very own bakery where she would make pies, cakes, and pastries to her heart's content. Just like her mama, she would bake love into each and every one. Because everyone knew that love, mixed with melt-in-your-mouth desserts, conquered all. Some of Noelle's happiest memories were sitting in the kitchen of her family's ranch house laughing and eating with her big, loving family.

Besides owning a bakery and becoming a social media influencer, getting married and starting a big family was number three on Noelle's to-do list. She longed for a country kitchen with a scarred oak harvest table that had been passed down for generations. A table big enough to seat her parents, her five sisters and their husbands, and a slew of cute kids. Sitting at the head of that table would be the love of Noelle's life, the sweet, honest man who made her heart swoon with just one flash of his dimpled smile.

She blinked.

Dimpled?

No, no dimples. Just one flash of his nice, dimple-less smile. A smile that held no guile. A smile that hadn't been given to every woman who looked his way. A smile reserved for only his beloved wife.

Unfortunately, finding that man hadn't been

easy. Noelle had dated a lot of toads on her way to finding her prince. Not that they had all been toads. Some had been perfectly nice guys . . . just not perfect for her. One thing or another had brought a screeching halt to her happily-ever-after dream.

Her college sweetheart, Randall, decided to go on a health kick and give up white sugar and flour right when she had decided she wanted to go to culinary school and become a pastry chef. And she couldn't marry a man who didn't love her baking. Then there was Michael. Sweet, loving Michael. He had it all . . . except a strong work ethic. He'd slept most of the day, occasionally played drums in a band at night, and was quite happy letting her pay all the bills. Luc was a sexy pastry chef. Everything had been going fine until he made fun of her pie baking, calling it simple country cuisine. Simple country cuisine! George had loved her pies a little too much. He'd gained thirty pounds while they'd been dating until his family had called an intervention and begged him to break up with her. She had been ready to call it quits, anyway. George was nice, but he hadn't been the one.

And Kenny—no, she refused to even think about Kenny.

Which was another reason she'd wanted to get out of Dallas. She wanted to forget that last humiliating night with Kenny. After being bullied as a kid, Noelle was good at pushing humiliating thoughts out of her head.

Once she closed out the cash register, wiped

off the tables, and put the last of the dishes in the dishwasher and started it, she freshened up her makeup, applied her favorite crimson-red lip stain and matching gloss, put on her favorite holly Christmas apron—because, as far as she was concerned, the Christmas holiday started right after Halloween—and got her tripod cellphone holder with the LED ring light that highlighted her complexion and slimmed her face.

Not that her face was fat, but she had gotten her Mimi's round cheeks and curvy body. When paired with her mama's short stature that she'd inherited, she could look a little . . . fuller.

Once she set her cellphone up on the prep island in the kitchen, she went about collecting the ingredients for her piecrust. She'd decided to start with the piecrust tonight and then do a pie a night until Thanksgiving. She always prepped everything before she started filming because, unlike most of the other social media chefs, she did all her posts live. Her followers seemed to love it when she dropped eggshells into the batter and had to fish them out or forgot an ingredient or overbrowned butter. Being imperfect made them think of her as more of a friend than a snooty chef.

That's how she felt too. She felt like she had close to four thousand friends sitting in the kitchen with her while she baked.

She loved it.

"Hey, y'all!" She smiled and waved at the image of herself on the cellphone screen. She looked pretty good if she did say so herself. She'd had her dark hair cut short a few months back and she loved the way it framed her face and made her green eyes look even bigger. "I hope y'all are doing well tonight. I've been busy selling muffins all day. Let me tell you . . . if you're ever in Wilder, Texas, you need to stop by Nothin' But Muffins. Sheryl Ann's muffins are the best in the world."

Numerous hearts and comments popped up on the screen.

I love a good muffin!
You're so lucky to get to bake muffins all day!
I'd love to try your muffin. (winky emoji)

Most people would have ignored the last comment, but Noelle had discovered ignoring wasn't the best way to handle her obnoxious followers.

"Now, Regular Joe, I've talked to you about this before. I don't put up with sexual innuendos on my posts. So if you can't rein it in, I'm going to have to block you. And you wouldn't want that, would you? Especially when some of your comments make me believe that you have a deep-down love of baking. And speaking of what people love, tonight I'm going to be showing you how to make the best piecrust you've ever tasted in your life."

She leaned in closer. "I'm gonna tell you a little secret." She waggled a finger at her phone. "But only if you promise not to tell. The key to flaky piecrust is exchanging some of the butter for vegetable shortenin'." She wasn't surprised when comments and horrified emojis started popping up on her live video. "I know. I know. Most of you think that piecrust should only be made with butter. But exchanging just four tablespoons of butter for shortening is going to make your crusts—as my Mimi would say—just about the best thing you ever flipped a lip over. Just stick with me and I'll prove it."

The entire time she measured out ingredients and put them in a bowl, she chatted like she was talking to her best friends. She talked about how she'd grown up making pies with her mama. All the different-flavored pies she'd made in her life. The bad hair day she'd had the other day. And breaking a nail and not being able to find an emery board.

In the years she'd been doing social media, she'd discovered her followers loved hearing about her personal life as much as they loved watching her bake. This was proven after she'd finished cutting the shortening and butter into the flour and asked for questions. There were a few about how long to freeze the butter and shortening and if you could use a food processor instead of a pastry cutter and what size was pea size, but the majority were about Noelle's recent breakup.

Why did you break up with Kenny again? I thought he was the one.

Did your boyfriend fool around? Is that why you broke up with him and moved back home?

Men are pigs. You should have baked him a poisonous apple pie before you left Dallas.

And one from Regular Joe. *So you're single now? Because I'm single too. Not that I mean anything by that. Just saying.*

Noelle answered the baking questions first, then moved on to the personal ones.

"Like I told you before, my and Kenny's breakup was a mutual decision. We were compatible on a lot of levels, but there were a few we weren't." Or just one. One very important level. "And yes, I'm single now, but I'm in no hurry to get back into another relationship."

"Well, I'm sorry to hear that, Smelly Ellie. Talk about having my heart broken right in two."

Every muscle in Noelle's body tensed at the voice that came from behind her. She knew the voice with the annoying teasing tone. She knew the nickname that made her want to use the rolling pin as a murder weapon. And she knew the scent that enveloped her. A scent of horses and leather . . . and arrogant jackass.

She whirled around to tell the arrogant jackass to get the hell out of her kitchen, but in the process, she knocked the mixing bowl off the counter. She lunged for it. Unfortunately, she had never been the most graceful Holiday sister. In fact, she'd always been the clumsiest, the one who hadn't excelled at sports . . . or anything that took physical ability. So instead of catching the stainless-steel bowl, she juggled it in her hands for what felt like a lifetime before it tipped and dumped the entire contents of flour-coated butter and shortening all over her cute apron before crashing to the floor with a tinny clatter.

She looked down at the overturned bowl and what was left of her piecrust in stunned disbelief for only a second before her gaze snapped up to the cowboy nonchalantly leaning in the doorway of the kitchen. His black Stetson was tipped back, revealing his smug face.

"Oops."

Noelle had never hated anyone in her life except this man. This arrogant, obnoxious devil of a man who had made her life a living hell growing up. She didn't just hate him. She despised him. Loathed him with every fiber of her being. So much so she struggled to even put it into words.

"Y-Y-You . . ."

His eyebrows lifted. "Still have that stutter I see. Well, you don't need to rush things with me, honey. I've always liked to take things nice and slow." Then he did that thing he'd always done— the thing that had made all the girls in high school want to drop their panties and Noelle want to clock him in the head with her backpack. He got this innocent little boy look in his eyes and then chewed on his bottom lip like he hadn't meant anything sexual by what he'd just said. Why, he would never think anything sexual about a woman. He was just a good ol' boy who liked to take things nice and slow.

But Noelle knew better. She knew behind the innocent blue eyes was a horny womanizer who wanted to screw his way through the adult female population—not just of Wilder but of the world. She wasn't about to put up with his aww-shucks act.

"I don't stutter! I'm just struggling to find words vile enough to describe how much I hate you."

Casey Remington's grin got even bigger and the deep dimple in his right cheek popped as he pushed away from the doorframe. "Now how can you hate a man you've known all your life? A man who has tried to come to your rescue whenever you needed me. Like the time you got stuck on top of the monkey bars and couldn't get down."

She felt her face heat with anger. "You didn't help me then. You left me hanging."

"I believed I offered to help you and you declined."

"While you were laughing so hard everyone came running over to witness me hanging there with my panties showing."

"We were in kindergarten. I don't think anyone cared about seeing your Minnie Mouse panties, Ellie." He moved closer and reached out. "You got something right . . ." His fingers brushed her cheek and the feeling of revulsion—yes, it had to be revulsion that caused her heart to beat faster and her stomach to drop—had her taking a step back.

"Don't touch—" She cut off when she stepped in the butter and shortening mess covering the floor and her feet slipped out from under her. Before her head could bash into the marble prep counter, she was caught and pulled against a chest that felt as hard as marble.

But warmer.

Much warmer.

"I got you, Ellie," Casey's deep voice rumbled.

He did have her. One muscled arm was wrapped around her waist and the other curved over her back, his hand cradling her head to his hard chest. Beneath her ear, she could hear his quick breathing and the strong, steady thumping of his heart.

"You okay?"

She wasn't hurt, but she certainly wasn't okay. She'd always wondered how lobsters felt when they were dropped into boiling pots of hot water. Now she knew. She felt like she was being boiled alive. Heat consumed her and she couldn't seem to draw in a deep breath. She felt completely disoriented, like she used to feel when she wound up the swing in the old oak and let it spin until she was dizzy and slightly nauseous. And yet, she would do it again and again for that tummy-dropping experience of the world spinning past in a blur.

WHAT WAS HAPPENING?

"Ellie?" Casey took her arms in his ranch-rough hands and drew her away from him. She lifted her gaze to his face, expecting to see a smirk. But he wasn't smirking. His lips were tipped down in a frown and his eyes didn't hold one teasing sparkle. Although they still sparkled. They sparkled like the ocean in the Greek vacation sites that kept popping up on her social media feed. His blue irises looked like the pictures of sun-dappled, turquoise water that she had the undeniable desire to dive right into.

"Are you hurt?" he asked. "Did you hit your head on the counter?"

Had she? She didn't remember hitting her head, but she must have. Otherwise, why was she feeling all loopy and weird? Things grew even weirder when Casey lifted his hand and ran his fingers through her hair. It was like his calloused fingertips were flint and all the nerve endings in her scalp matches. He struck a tingling spark wherever he touched.

"I don't feel a lump, but I think we should take you to the county hospital anyway. You aren't acting like yourself." He scooped her up in his arms, and very few men had ever scooped her up in their arms. In fact, her daddy had been the only one and only when she'd been little. She wasn't little now. She might be short, but she wasn't what people had ever called petite. And yet, Casey lifted her as if she didn't weight more than a feather pillow.

Which made her stomach feel like a pillow—a pillow that had been ripped open and shaken so all the feathers went fluttering through the air. She was so stunned by her body's reaction that she didn't say a word as he headed out of the kitchen . . . until she glanced over his broad shoulder and saw her phone.

She was still live!

"Put me down!" She struggled until he set her on her feet, then she raced over to remove her phone from the tripod. There was a steady stream of comments. A few asking if they needed to call 911, but most asking about the hot cowboy hero who had just saved her life.

Noelle brushed the flour from her cheek and tried to salvage the situation.

"Sorry about that, y'all! I'm fine. Just fine. Unfortunately, it looks like my clumsiness has ruined the piecrust. But don't you worry. I'll be back tomorrow night to teach you that piecrust secret my mama taught me." She winked. "Because as y'all know, *there's always something bakin' in the* Holiday Kitchen." She tapped the live button to end the session and waited for her screen to reset before she released her smile and her breath.

"Always something bakin' in the *Holiday Kitchen?*"

The smirk in Casey's voice was back. When she turned, there was the arrogant, obnoxious man she loathed. The concern she'd read in his eyes had obviously been a trick of the bright kitchen lights. And the strange reaction to his touch just . . . she didn't know what it had been. All she knew was that it would never be repeated. At least not if she could help it.

"Get out," she growled.

The smirk on his face deepened. "I guess you're okay."

She picked up the rolling pin and moved toward him. "I said get out."

He took a step back and his eyes twinkled. "Now is this any way to treat the man who just rescued you from a cracked skull?"

"Get out!"

He laughed his annoying laugh. "Anything you say, Smelly Ellie. Anything you say." He turned and walked out of the kitchen.

Since she didn't trust him as far as she could throw him, she followed him. Once he stepped out the door, she quickly took the keys from her jeans pocket and locked it, mentally chastising herself for not locking it before she started her social media post. She wouldn't make that mistake twice.

There were scoundrels in Wilder, Texas.

Her brow knitted as she watched Casey strut to his truck.

Scoundrels who could make a gal feel like a cooked lobster.

Chapter Two

Casey felt a little out of sorts after he left Nothin' But Muffins, but he figured it wasn't anything a cold beer and a pretty country girl looking for a good time wouldn't fix. He had always believed happiness was something you had to work for. It wasn't just handed out like trick-or-treat candy. And he worked hard at being the happy-go-lucky man he was and not sweating the small stuff. Or the big stuff for that matter, something his daddy had never been too happy about.

Sam Remington loved to sweat, both literally and figuratively. He worked from before sunrise to well after sunset and believed his two sons should too. He worried about everything. Cattle prices, drought, Hank Holiday's ranch being more successful than his, Casey never growing up. The latter was probably something to worry about, but Casey flat refused to spend his life worrying and working. If something came up that took him a little by surprise, he dealt with it.

As he drove his truck to the Hellhole bar, he had to admit the feel of Noelle in his arms had taken him a little by surprise. Or maybe what had taken him by surprise was the reaction his body had to the feel of her in his arms.

It had liked holding her. It had liked holding her a lot.

Which confused Casey no small amount.

Noelle Holiday had never been his type.

He preferred a tall woman he could look right in the eyes without getting a crick in his neck. He preferred blue eyes to eyes the color of fungus growing in the cracks of a dead tree. He preferred blondes, redheads, or brunettes—even purple and pink—to hair the color of a black widow.

He also preferred women who enjoyed a little teasing and a good joke. Noelle Holiday was as sour and driven as his daddy and never had been able to take a joke. Which probably explained why he worked so hard to get under both their skins. The only thing he enjoyed more than riling his daddy was watching Noelle's eyes squint with anger and her cheeks turn a mottled red.

Which was exactly how she'd looked after he'd startled her and she'd dumped whatever she'd been making all over herself. He'd been thoroughly enjoying himself. . . until she'd slipped and almost cracked her head open on the marble counter. Then he'd been scared. Like heart-pounding, nerve-jumping scared.

His fear probably explained why he'd gotten a semi-erection while holding her close. Emotions were complicated things that could easily get confused. His mama and daddy's relationship was a perfect example of that. They had thought they were in love, but it turned out they didn't even like each other enough to share custody of their two sons. Mama left when Casey was no more than two and never looked back. Which probably explained why Casey didn't trust relationships as far as he could throw them. He kept his dealings with women simple and purely sexual.

And he was NOT sexually interested in Noelle Holiday.

To prove, it, not more than fifteen minutes later, he was bellied up to the bar at the Hellhole enjoying a beer and scoping out a pretty blonde sitting at a table not more than a few feet from the bar. He sent her a smile when she glanced over and was a little taken back when her eyes widened with surprise. Not good surprise, but shocked surprise. Did he have something on his face?

He turned to the mirror behind the bar, but he didn't see anything unusual. When he turned back around, the blonde was talking to her friends. They all turned to look at him before glancing back at the cellphone the blonde was holding.

Maybe they thought he looked like someone they knew. Some folks thought he looked like that cocky fighter pilot in the second *Top Gun* movie. Casey didn't see the resemblance, but if women thought he looked like a movie star, who was he to argue.

"Checking out your prospects for the evening?"

He pulled his gaze away from the women and saw Fiona Stokes standing there in her antiquated business suit and mangy mink stole. Mrs. Stokes was the matriarch of the town. Her family had started Wilder and she pretty much owned half the businesses—including the bank. She was tough as nails and never minced words and Casey pretty much adored the hell out of her.

"Well, it looks like my prospects just improved." He winked. "What do you say, beautiful? You want to spend the evening with a lonely cowboy?"

A smile quivered on her thin lips for a second before they returned to a stern line. "Don't waste that boyish charm on me, Casey Remington. I'm too old for it."

"You're not old. You're just mature." He helped her up on the barstool. "Bourbon?"

"What else?"

He grinned as he motioned to the bartender and pointed at Mrs. Stokes. Everyone in Wilder knew Mrs. Stokes drank straight bourbon. She also smoked like a chimney. Or had until a few weeks ago when Corbin Whitlock had talked her into quitting. Casey was still trying to figure out what he had on the old gal. Whatever it was, she wasn't telling. So he'd taken to guessing.

"You once worked at Mrs. Fields Boardinghouse as a lovely lady of the evening and Corbin is threatening to reveal your sordid past if you don't give up smoking."

She cocked an eyebrow. "I wish I'd been smart enough to get paid for having sex with men. If I had been, I'd be filthy rich rather than just rich."

He laughed. "You're my kind of woman, Ms. Stokes."

"If I was forty years younger, I'd give you a run for your money. You need a strong woman who won't put up with your shenanigans."

"But shenanigans are so much fun."

Her eyes twinkled and she swatted him on the arm. "You are a bad boy. But all bad boys must grow up. When exactly do you plan to do that?"

"Now, Ms. Stokes, don't go sounding like my daddy. All he can talk about is me settling down. But I'm not ready to settle down just yet. In fact, I might not ever be ready." He winked at her. "I might be like you and just play the field."

"That certainly wasn't by choice. I wanted to settle down, but my husbands kept dying off. Now, I'm stuck with remaining single or marrying a man who is content to sit in his recliner all day and watch *The Price is Right*. Or a younger man who is after my money more than my heart. You, on the other hand, have a wide array of women to settle down with." She glanced at the women at the table. "Those three seem to be quite smitten with you. Although I'd prefer you chose a Wilder woman."

He was about to reiterate he wasn't interested in choosing any woman for a wife when Melba Wadley stepped up with a big basket hooked over her arm. He didn't even have to look to know what was inside. Melba fostered orphaned or abused animals. She always had one or two she was looking to find homes for.

"Hey, y'all. I'm glad I ran into you, Casey." She lifted the basket up to the bar and two furry heads popped out—one golden and the other black.

"I'd like you to meet June Carter and Johnny Cash." Melba named all her foster animals after country singers.

Casey couldn't help lavishing ear scratches on the two cute Lab puppies. "Hey, Junie. Hey, John. How adorable are y'all?" He glanced at Melba to see her smiling like she'd just struck a deal. "But sorry, Mel. Like I told you before, I can't take them. If I bring home any more animals, besides ones who will make us a profit, Daddy will tan my hide and hang it out to dry."

"How about one puppy? They would make fine hunting dogs. Or maybe you could give them as a gift." Melba shot him a sly look. "They'll melt a woman's heart in a New York second."

"I'm sure they will." He laughed as the black puppy licked his face and made his own heart melt. "But I'm not looking to melt any women's hearts. But I will talk to my daddy about getting a couple hunting dogs. He does love to hunt."

Melba's face lit up. "That's great! Just call me at the sheriff's office and let me know." Her gaze shifted to something behind Casey and she grinned. "For now, it looks like you don't need puppies to get women." He turned to see the blonde and her two friends standing there.

"Come on, Mel," Mrs. Stokes said as she accepted the bourbon from the bartender and got off the stool. "Let's not cramp the young buck's style."

He watched them walk off before he turned to the women and flashed a smile. "Good evenin', ladies."

"Sorry to interrupt," the blonde said. "But you look familiar."

His smile got bigger. "I love being familiar."

She laughed. "No, really. Were you at Nothin' But Muffins tonight?"

He blinked. "I was, but I'm sorry. I don't remember seeing y'all there." He knew for a fact they hadn't been there. The only woman there had been the one who hated his guts.

The blonde turned to her friends. "I told you it was him." She turned back to Casey with a big smile. "I just wanted to say that I love *Holiday Kitchen* and I think it's so great Noelle has finally found a man like you. It just gives the rest of us hope that one day we'll find our own cowboy hero to walk in and sweep us off our feet."

Casey was normally never at a loss for words, but he was at a loss now. "Umm . . . I'm sorry, but I'm afraid I don't know what y'all are talking about."

The blonde looked confused. "So you didn't save Noelle from falling?"

Casey stared at her. "How do you know about that?"

She tapped her cellphone and held it out so he could see the screen. Noelle's face had him taking a step back. He had thought cutting her hair short had been a bad idea, but now he had to admit that it didn't look half bad. She looked a little like Snow White with her pale skin, red lipstick, and ruffled apron.

An apron he'd seen just that night.

Suddenly, it dawned on him what he was looking at. He was looking at the video Noelle had been making when he'd walked into the Nothin' But Muffins kitchen. He thought for sure she'd delete it—or at least edit him out. But not more than a minute later, his voice came out of the blonde's phone.

"Well, I'm sorry to hear that, Smelly Ellie. Talk about having my heart broken right in two."

Noelle whirled around and struggled to catch the bowl she'd knocked off. Once it hit the floor, he remembered the hate in her eyes. But with her back turned to the camera, he couldn't see it now. Nor could he hear what she was saying. The only voice he could hear was his own. He'd been teasing her, but without her sassy replies, it sounded more like he was flirting with her. Then she stepped back and slipped. As she started to fall, his face popped into the screen. A face of sheer panic. It settled into relief when he caught her and pulled her into his chest.

And what the hell was that expression on his face when he drew back and looked down at her?

"It's just so sweet," the brunette gushed. "Noelle has been looking for love and she didn't realize it was right in her backyard." She pressed a hand to her chest. "She didn't realize you've had a crush on her since kindergarten."

His eyes widened and he shook his head. "Sorry, ladies, but I'm afraid that y'all have gotten the wrong idea. I don't have a crush on Noelle Holiday. I've never had a crush on her. She slipped and fell and I—"

"Was worried sick," the blonde finished. "It's written all over your face."

He frowned and tried to get ahold of the situation. "Okay. I get that it looked like that. And to be honest, I never want to see someone get hurt. But I'm not interested in Noelle. And if she were here right now, she'd tell you that she's certainly not interested in me." He tipped his hat. "Now if y'all will excuse me."

When he got in his truck, he tossed his hat to the dashboard and released his breath in a frustrated huff. This night hadn't turned out quite like he'd planned. He should have never stopped when he saw the lights on at Nothin' But Muffins. But he knew Sheryl Ann was out of town and worried someone had broken in. Now he was paying for doing his civic duty.

Maybe that's exactly what Noelle wanted. She wanted him to pay for all the teasing he'd done over the years. But harmless teasing was one thing. Posting embarrassing videos on social media for the entire world to see was another. While he wanted to ignore what she'd done and move on, he couldn't.

He started his truck, popped it into drive, and sprayed gravel as he left the Hellhole's parking lot. He drove past Nothin' But Muffins first. When he saw it was dark, he headed for Holiday Ranch.

The ranch was much smaller than Remington Ranch, but the two-story farmhouse with its huge porch had always been much homier than the sterile house Casey had grown up in. Although now that his brother, Rome, had married Cloe Holiday things were changing. The Holiday women seemed to know how to make a house a home. Cloe had filled the inside of the Remington house with throw pillows, comfy blankets, scented candles, and framed photographs. On the outside, she'd covered the front porch with as many pumpkins, dried cornstalks, and autumn wreathes as her family's porch. The wreath on the Holidays' front door was so full of artificial leaves, tiny pumpkins, and little stuffed scarecrows that Casey struggled to find a place to knock.

And maybe he shouldn't knock.

He glanced at the dark windows. He didn't want to wake up the entire household. Especially when he knew Hank owned a shotgun. Even though his daughter had married Rome, Hank still struggled with the grudge he'd harbored for decades against the Remingtons.

Not wanting his butt to be filled with buckshot, Casey turned from the door and headed down the porch steps. He knew where Noelle and Hallie's childhood bedroom was located. Once he got around back, he picked up a few pebbles from the ground and tossed them up at the window. He was starting to think he was wasting his time when the window opened.

But it wasn't Noelle who peeked her head out.

It was Jace Carson.

Like Casey, Jace had been born and raised in Wilder. Unlike Casey, he'd moved away after high school to become a pro football player. A career-ending shoulder injury had brought him back home again where he'd fallen in love with Noelle's sister, Hallie, and married her. Just a few weeks ago in fact. Which might explain the scowl on his face.

"Casey?"

Casey lifted a hand. "Hey, Jace." He was about to explain what he was doing there when Hallie's voice drifted out the window.

"What are you doing, baby? Don't tell me I was too hot for you and you needed a little cool air."

Casey cringed. "Uhh . . . I'll just come back later, Jace." He started to leave, but Hallie popped her head out next to Jace's.

"Casey?"

He lifted a hand. "Hey, Hal." He had always gotten along with the other Holiday sisters. It was just Noelle who hated him.

"Is something wrong?" Her eyes widened. "Is Cloe having the baby?"

He quickly shook his head. "No, no, Cloe's fine. I just stopped by to see Noelle."

Hallie's eyes widened even more. "Noelle?"

The window next to Jace and Hallie's opened and Mimi peeked her head out. "What is the world is going—Casey Remington?"

He sighed. "Hi, Miss Mimi. Before you get worried, this has nothing to do with Cloe."

"He says he's here to see Noelle," Hallie said.

"Noelle?" Mimi looked at him as if he'd sprouted horns.

Not wanting the rest of the Holidays to stick their heads out the windows, he decided it was time to leave. "Sorry to bother y'all. I'll just come back in the morning to talk with Noelle."

He turned and headed for his truck. But before he could reach it, the front door opened and Noelle stepped out. Her hair was mussed and her green eyes snapped with anger as she stomped down the porch steps. But it was hard to be too intimidated when she was dressed in a candy cane onesie. If not for the full-figured curves outlined by the fuzzy material, she'd look like an angry dark-haired toddler.

"Just why are you stalking me, Casey Remington?"

"Stalking is a pretty strong word, Ellie. Especially when I think you know exactly why I'm here. I don't find your revenge amusing."

She stopped in front of him and he got a whiff of her scent. Ever since he could remember, Noelle had always smelled like cookies straight from the oven. Yummy, warm homemade cookies. "Revenge? What are you talking about?"

He ignored the tempting scent and stayed focused on the problem at hand. "I'm talking about the video you posted of me on social media."

"I didn't post a video of you. I posted a video of me and you just happened to videobomb it."

"You could have edited me out."

"Not when it was live."

He stared at her. "Live?"

"Yes. Live. I always film live."

So she hadn't posted it on purpose. But that

didn't make things better. "Can you take it down?"

"I already did. The last thing I need is my followers thinking you're my new boyfriend."

"Ditto. Nice jammies, by the way." His gaze swept over the onesie. The fabric looked cuddly soft . . . or maybe what looked cuddly soft were the full breasts and hips beneath. He realized he was ogling her and quickly lifted his gaze. Even with her back to the porch light, he could see the blush staining her cheeks.

"I'm sure you prefer your women to wear itchy, uncomfortable lingerie."

He did. Which didn't explain the warm pool of desire that settled in his stomach at just the thought of cuddling up next to the cozy pajama-wearing woman in front of him. He blinked the strange thought away as she continued.

"Now if you're done waking up my entire family, you need to go. You're not welcome at Holiday Ranch."

At one time, that had been true. Hank and Sam had been sworn enemies since before Casey had been born and their offspring had not been welcome on either's ranch. But times had changed. Something Casey couldn't help pointing out as he headed to his truck.

"Well, that's interesting because your mama invited me to Thanksgiving dinner. And how can I refuse when . . ." He flashed a smile over his shoulder and winked. "'There's always something cookin' in the *Holiday Kitchen*.'"

Chapter Three

When Noelle got back upstairs after talking with Casey, she wasn't surprised to find Mimi waiting for her. Her grandmother had always enjoyed meddling in her granddaughters' lives. Especially if it had to do with the Remington brothers.

Regardless of the Remington-Holiday feud, Mimi had always had her eye on the brothers as mates for her granddaughters. Probably because Casey and Rome were successful ranchers and Mimi would do just about anything to make Holiday Ranch succeed.

"So it looks like you and Casey have finally figured out there's more to all that teasing and anger than meets the eye." Mimi had always thought Casey's teasing and Noelle's hatred of that teasing hid a much stronger emotion.

She was wrong.

Nothing was stronger than Noelle's hate for Casey.

"Not hardly, Mimi. As far as I'm concerned, he's still an arrogant jack—butt." Her grandmother didn't put up with cussing, unless it was from her.

"So don't be trying to match me up with him like you matched up Rome and Cloe."

Her grandmother's eyes twinkled. "I'd say that worked out pretty well."

It had. Cloe and Rome were as happy as two bugs in a rug.

"Rome and Cloe worked out because they have mutual respect for each other. I don't have a speck of respect for Casey."

"I don't know why not. Underneath that charming teaser is a damn fine rancher and a good man."

"Rome is the damn fine rancher and a good man. Casey just pretends to be a rancher when there isn't a beer or a woman around."

Mimi chuckled. "Nothing wrong with a young man sowing his wild oats."

"He's not only sowed them, he's burned down the entire field. And I'm not looking for an arrogant, irresponsible man who can't keep his pants zipped."

Mimi studied her. "Is that what happened with Kenny? He couldn't keep his pants zipped?"

That hadn't been the problem at all. In fact, it had been the exact opposite. Kenny had had no problem zipping his pants up . . . after Noelle pretty much offered herself up on a silver platter.

"I don't want to talk about Kenny, Mimi. He's water under the bridge. Nor do I want to talk about Casey. He showed up here tonight because of a misunderstanding. Believe me, he would never come courting."

"If I've learned anything in life, it's never say

never." With a smug smile, Mimi turned and headed to her room.

Noelle sighed and went back to bed. Although it took her a while to get to sleep. Her mind kept returning to the weird emotions she'd experienced while in Casey's arms. After staying up until well after midnight, morning came much too quickly.

Getting up at the crack of dawn was the worst part of covering for Sheryl Ann. Nothin' But Muffins opened at seven o'clock in the morning and the muffins and coffee needed to be ready before then. Which meant Noelle had to get up at five so she could be out the door by six. Once she was showered and dressed, she headed downstairs to say goodbye to whoever was up.

She stepped into the kitchen and froze when she discovered her parents locked in a passionate embrace. It wasn't like she hadn't seen her mama and daddy kiss before, but it had been a while and never quite as R-rated. Embarrassed, she quickly ducked back out. She was so distracted that she walked out the front door without paying attention and ran right into the cowboy standing on the porch.

"Whoa there." His hands closed around her arms to steady her.

She stared at the muscled chest beneath the flannel shirt for a second before lifting her gaze . . . to the handsomest cowboy she'd ever seen in her life. She tried not to stare, but it was impossible.

Gah, the man was gorgeous.

"You must be Noelle." He held out a hand. "I'm Reid Mitchell, the new ranch hand."

She snapped out of her daze. "Oh! Reid Mitchell." She took his hand and pumped it awkwardly. "My family has told me all about you." Not all about him. They hadn't mentioned how hot he was. When Hallie had told her how long Reid had been cowboying, she'd pictured a middle-aged man with a weathered face and a bushy handlebar mustache. She had not pictured a man no older than mid-thirties with just enough scruff and eye crinkles to look ruggedly sexy.

"Well, I hope it was all good," he said.

"Good enough for me to know that you're much more than a ranch hand."

He blushed. He actually blushed. Who was this man? And please, God, make him single.

"Good mornin', Reid!" Hallie stepped out the door. "I see you've met my little sister."

"We just met." Noelle shot Hallie a why-didn't-you-tell-me-about-hiring-a-hot-cowboy look. Hallie read it perfectly because she grinned widely and thumped Noelle on the arm.

"You're welcome." She looked at Reid. "You ready to head to Austin and pick out a bull? I thought we'd stop off and get some muffins first."

"Muffins!" Noelle exclaimed as she raced to her car.

Thankfully, she had enough muffins left over from the day before to fill all the morning orders, including Hallie's and Reid's. Reid's order made him even more appealing. He didn't blink when he ordered a Red Velvet Valentine muffin with cute pink heart sprinkles covering the cream cheese frosting. Since red velvet was her favorite cake flavor, she couldn't help feeling like it was a sign. After some careful prying, she discovered he *was* single and raising his teenage niece. Which was just another check in the wowza! column.

By the time he and Hallie left, Noelle had to wonder if maybe there was another reason fate had brought her home. A tall, dark, and handsome reason.

Around noon, customers slowed way down. So Noelle headed to the kitchen and started baking. She mixed up numerous batters of the most popular muffins. Since she had worked for Sheryl Ann during high school, she knew all the recipes by heart. In fact, she was probably the only one who knew them. Sheryl Ann was extremely secretive about her muffin recipes. It showed how much she trusted Noelle that she'd shared them with her. She had even asked her to come up with a new muffin recipe for the holiday season. Fa-La-La Fruitcake hadn't sold well for the past few Christmases.

After putting the muffins into the commercial-sized oven, she walked into the pantry to see if she could find an ingredient that would be the perfect star of a holiday muffin. Ginger and cinnamon seemed too predictable. Molasses a little too strong. She wanted a muffin that made people think of happy holiday memories with each bite. She was still going through the spice rack when she glanced up and saw the artificial tree box and large storage container labeled *Christmas decorations*.

Decorating was something else Noelle had inherited from her mama. She had always loved decorating. Especially for Christmas. She didn't hesitate to grab the stepladder so she could retrieve the boxed tree and large container.

She set the tree up in the corner of the window and then opened the container and pulled out the lights and decorations, which consisted of cute little glass ornaments of cakes, donuts, pies, and cupcakes covered in sparkly glitter. In between decorating, she waited on the occasional customer. Once she finished the tree, she decided to put the leftover garland and lights around the front windows.

Unfortunately, the windows were so tall she couldn't reach the top even with the stepladder—just one of the many challenges of being five foot nothing. She was teetering on the ladder on her tiptoes with her arms stretched over her head when the bell on the door jingled and a deep voice sent a shiver through her body.

"Whatcha doin', shorty?"

She whipped around so fast she lost her balance. Once again, she found herself being rescued by Casey Remington. Only this time, he didn't catch her as much as break her fall. She fell straight into him and they both ended up on the floor—her on top and him on the bottom. It took a full minute to recover her senses. When she did, those senses seemed to be completely focused on one thing.

The man lying beneath her.

His masculine scent wrapped around her like a Yankee candle set ablaze and his muscles flexed beneath her from her breasts to the inside of her thighs cradling his lean hips. In the very center of those lean hips, she felt another muscle. An extremely impressive muscle that nudged the spot between her legs and woke it up with a zing that had her sucking in her breath and sitting straight up.

Which did nothing to help the situation. Now she was straddling that impressive muscle and causing even more zings to rocket through her. When her gaze snapped to Casey's, it looked like he felt them too. His Grecian-ocean eyes held confusion and . . . a whole lot of heat. Heat that had her insides melting like a pat of butter on hot yeast rolls.

Before she could freak out—or do something really stupid like rub against his impressive hardness like a dog in heat—the bell jingled and both their gazes snapped to the door as Mrs. Stokes walked in. She didn't even blink when she saw them. Almost as if she'd always known she'd walk in on such a scene.

Noelle quickly got to her feet and tried to act like she hadn't just been straddling Casey Remington like her favorite rocking horse. It was difficult to do considering her body felt like a commercial cooktop set on high.

"Good afternoon, Ms. Stokes. What can I get you?"

Mrs. Stokes glanced at Casey, who was now

standing with his cowboy hat shielding the part of him Noelle had been straddling. "I'd say 'I'll have what you're having,' but I'm too old to be rolling around on the floor. So just get me a Pumpkin Harvest muffin and hot tea with plenty of honey."

"Yes, ma'am." Noelle hurried to the counter to fill the order and was relieved when she turned back around after filling a cup with hot water to find Casey gone.

"Was it hot?"

Mrs. Stokes's question pulled Noelle's gaze away from the door and she tried to explain. "I'm afraid you got the wrong idea, Ms. Stokes. I fell off the ladder while putting up Christmas lights and Casey just happened to walk in and catch me—or not catch as much as break my fall. It was just an accident."

Mrs. Stokes took the cup from her. "I was talking about the tea. Last time, the water was more lukewarm."

"Oh . . . uh, yes, ma'am. I'm sure it's hot."

Mrs. Stokes nodded. "Good. I hate lukewarm anything. And just for the record. I never much believed in accidents. Just fate." She sniffed. "I think something's burning."

"The muffins!" Noelle raced into the kitchen to discover all the muffins had burned.

She spent the rest of the day making more. By closing, she was exhausted and she still had her piecrust post to do. But she couldn't let her followers down. So after making sure the front door was locked, she fixed her makeup, put on a cute apron with a Santa Claus print, and prepped the ingredients before she pulled her cellphone from her purse.

It was the first opportunity she'd had to look at it all day. She opened the social media app and then pulled up her profile page. The phone almost slipped from her fingers when she saw her number of followers.

Thirty-nine thousand five hundred and fifty-seven!

She glanced up at her profile picture to make sure she had the right page, then back at the number—a number that kept increasing even as she watched. Thirty-nine thousand five hundred and fifty-eight. Fifty-nine. Sixty. It got all the way to thirty-nine thousand six hundred before she realized what was happening.

"Holy crap! I'm trending."

But how? And why?

As soon as she clicked on her notifications, she had her answer. She was tagged in a long line of posts—posts of the video she'd deleted. Or tried to delete. It looked like some of her followers had downloaded it and reposted. Those posts had been reposted until the video had gone viral with hashtags like #thecowboyandthebaker #bakinguparomance #lovescookingintheholidaykitchen #childhoodcrush #allIwantforchristmasisacowboyhero

"Oh my God."

She had to fix this. She had to fix this now.

She quickly attached her cellphone to the tripod, smoothed her hair, and plastered on a smile before she tapped the live button that started the post.

"Hey, y'all. I promised I would get back to my mama's piecrust recipe and here I am. But before we get started, I wanted to talk a little about my last post. I guess it sent everyone into a tizzy. But I wanted to let everyone know that—" Before she could finish the screen filled with an explosion of hearts and cowboy emojis and comments. She had so many she couldn't read them fast enough, but she was still able to get the gist.

Everyone was thrilled she had found herself a new boyfriend.

And not just any boyfriend, but a cowboy hero who'd had a crush on her since kindergarten.

She sat there stunned, taking in all the comments and emoji love. She couldn't help the flood of pure endorphins that enveloped her. As the youngest of six siblings, she'd always had to fight for attention—always had to fight to be seen and heard. But now she was seen and heard . . . and liked.

Liked a lot.

She felt like Sally Field after winning her second academy award, "*. . . you like me. Right now, you like me!*" And she knew if she told her almost forty thousand followers the truth there was a good chance all their likes and love would be gone in a cotton-pickin' minute. She didn't want that to happen. Forty thousand was a seriously big number. She followed numerous social media chefs with lower numbers who had gotten paid sponsors. If she could get some sponsors, she might be able to make *Holiday Kitchen* her full-time job. She might even have the social media clout to get a cookbook on a bestsellers' list, which would give her the money she needed to finance her own bakery.

And what would it hurt if she didn't explain things? What would it hurt if she just played along for a little while? Just until she could win all her new followers over with her baking ability. Once she hooked them, she would simply say that she and Casey hadn't worked out. Which was the truth. She and Casey would never work out. And it wasn't like he didn't owe her after all the teasing and bullying he'd done.

This was the perfect way to pay him back and do a little teasing of her own.

Looking directly into the camera, she smiled. "I just wanted to let y'all know that . . . I'm just in seventh heaven! I mean who wouldn't be after a handsome cowboy sweeps you off your feet. I'd love to tell you more, but with Thanksgiving right around the corner, we need to get to that piecrust recipe. You can't have a great Thanksgiving without pie!" She winked. "Or a hot cowboy hero."

Chapter Four

SOMETHING WAS WRONG.

Something was definitely wrong.

Casey couldn't quite put his finger on why, but he didn't feel at all like himself. He felt grumpy and cranky. And Casey had never been grumpy and cranky in his life. Rome, yes. His daddy, most definitely. But Casey could always find a rainbow even on the rainiest of days.

But for the last couple days, there were no rainbows to be found. He felt . . . depressed. And nothing seemed to help. Not morning rides on his Appaloosa horse, Domino. Not hanging in the barn with the family goat, the dogs and cats, and the new litter of kittens. Not an extra helping of Cloe's coffee cake at breakfast. Not herding cattle with Rome. Not even finishing the cradle he'd spent the last few months making.

In fact, placing the cradle in his niece's room made him feel even more depressed.

There was something about seeing the cradle that made him feel . . . empty. Like his life was definitely missing a piece of the puzzle. Which was ridiculous. He didn't want kids. He'd never wanted kids.

But if that were true, why did a huge lump form in his throat when Cloe gave the cradle a push and it slowly rocked back and forth?

"Oh, Casey." Tears flooded her eyes as she pressed her hands to her chest. "It's just perfect."

Casey swallowed down the lump and gave his sister-in-law a hug. "Hey now, no tears. If Rome finds out I made you cry, he'll kick my butt."

She hugged him back before she stepped away with a stern look. "If he kicks your butt, I'll kick his. No one messes with my little brother. Not even my beloved husband." She studied him with eyes the exact shade of green that had been plaguing his thoughts for the last few days. "So you want to tell me what's been going on with you?"

He started to play dumb, but then changed his mind. He wanted to figure out what was going on with him too and maybe Cloe could help.

"I don't know. I just haven't felt like myself lately."

"Rome and I have noticed you've been a little out of sorts. Did something happen?"

The question immediately brought up images of Noelle straddling him. Yes, something had happened. Something he definitely couldn't talk about with Noelle's older sister. He didn't even want to think about it. And yet, he couldn't seem to think about anything else. Every time he turned around, Noelle's green eyes flashed into his brain. Green eyes filled with sexual heat.

He mentally shook himself. No, he had to be mistaken. She had never been interested in him. Especially sexually.

Unfortunately, there was no mistaking that he'd been sexually interested in her. Even now, just the thought of her full-figured body pressed against him made him semi-erect. He quickly turned away from Cloe and pretended to be examining the cradle for flaws while he got his libido in check. His sister-in-law's next question had him wondering if she could read minds.

"Have you met a girl?"

"No!" He whirled around. "Why would you ask that?"

She shrugged. "Developing feelings for someone can make you feel out of sorts. There's not someone you've met recently that maybe you want to get more serious with?"

"You know I don't do serious, Cloe."

A soft smile lifted the corners of her mouth. "I know you don't want to do serious, Casey. But sometimes love sneaks up on you when you least expect it."

He laughed at just the thought of being in love with Noelle. "Believe me, it's not love." Lust maybe. But definitely not love.

Maybe that was the problem. With all the ranch work, weddings, and cradle making, he hadn't had much leftover time for his own personal needs. He'd had a heavy make-out session with Sissy Haskins's cousin at Hallie and Jace's wedding . . . before Noelle had shown up and ruined things. But he hadn't had sex in a while and that could make any man in his prime feel depressed and apt to get over stimulated. Even by a woman who hated him.

The revelation made Casey feel better.

He just needed to relieve some sexual tension and everything would go back to normal. Since tonight was the Wednesday before Thanksgiving, the biggest bar night of the year, Casey had an extremely good chance of doing just that.

"Where did you get the cradle?"

Casey turned to see his father standing in the doorway.

Sam Remington wasn't big in stature. Both Casey and Rome were taller and broader shouldered. But that didn't stop Sam from commanding any room he stepped into. Probably because he was like a dark cloud blocking out all the sunshine with his grumpy demeanor.

"Casey made it for the baby," Cloe said. "Isn't it perfect?"

Sam walked over and examined the cradle, running his hand over the pine Casey had painstakingly sanded. "It could use a coat of paint."

Leave it to his father to find a flaw.

Cloe hooked her arm through Casey's. "I don't agree. I think the natural look is much prettier than paint. I'm just tickled pink with it and I know Baby Girl Remington will be too." She leaned up and kissed Casey on the cheek. "Now I better go check on dinner. You'll be here, won't you, Case? It's chicken potpie. Your favorite."

"Everything you make is my favorite," he said.

"But I'm going to have to pass. I have plans to head to the Hellhole."

She laughed. "Of course you do. I'll be sure to save you one." She headed for the door, but then stopped before she got there and pointed a finger between him and Sam. "I'm setting up a rule right now. No arguing in the baby's room."

It was a good rule. If anyone liked to argue, it was Casey and his father. Mainly because they both knew what buttons to push to piss each other off. This was proven as soon as Cloe left the room.

"The Hellhole?" Sam said. "Don't you think you're getting a little too old to go out carousing?"

The comment had Casey bristling, but he'd spent his life dealing with his daddy's disapproval and had learned how to keep his anger to himself and a carefree smile on his face.

"Nope. You're never too old to enjoy life. Something you seem to have forgotten."

"Enjoying life is one thing. Acting like an irresponsible fool is something else. You're twenty-four years old. It's time you started acting like a man instead of a childish boy. I was running this ranch all by myself when I was no more than nineteen."

Casey had heard these exact words so many times that they shouldn't hold any power over him. But damned if they didn't. That was how it worked when you only had the love of one parent. Even if you didn't want it to, what they thought about you mattered.

It mattered too much.

"You need to stop running around being a cowboy Casanova and start thinking about settling down and starting a family," Sam continued. "Which is why I invited Judge Matthews and his daughter, Melissa, over for dinner on Friday. Melissa just finished passing the bar. And a lawyer and a judge will make a perfect addition to this family."

Casey wasn't at all surprised. Sam had been dropping hints about him dating Melissa Matthews for months. He just hadn't thought he'd take matters into his own hands. Of course, he should have known better. Patience wasn't one of Sam's virtues.

"So you're arranging weddings now, Sam?" he said dryly. "A little archaic, isn't it? Even for an arrogant control freak like you."

Sam's eyes darkened and Casey figured he was about to get his ass chewed out. But Sam must have remembered Cloe's rule because he kept his voice even and his temper reined in.

"You need to watch it, Casey. I still run this ranch."

"With Rome's, Cloe's, and my help. Without us, you couldn't do it and you know it. So don't try to bend me to your will. I'm a grown man. As long as I pull my weight, it's none of your damn business what I do with my free time."

"You live in this house by my grace. Don't forget that."

"I live here by Rome's grace as well. He told

me you signed over half the business when Cloe got pregnant."

Sam's eyes narrowed. "If you marry Melissa and get her pregnant, I'll give you the other half to build your own house on. It's time you had a home of your own."

That hurt. Probably because it was true. He shouldn't be living with his brother and father, especially now that Rome's family was growing. He didn't doubt Rome and Cloe would have more children, which wouldn't leave room for a bachelor uncle.

"Everything okay in here?" Rome stepped into the room, no doubt sent by Cloe to make sure Sam and Casey were keeping things civil. But civility had never been Sam's strong suit.

"Maybe you can talk some sense into your brother, Rome," Sam said. "Lord knows I've never been able to." He turned and walked out of the room.

Rome looked at Casey. "I guess you two got into it again. I swear y'all love to get under each other's skin. What's going on now?"

"He's trying to marry me off to Melissa Matthews because he thinks a judge and lawyer in the family will come in handy."

"Melissa Matthews? Didn't you used to date her in college?"

"We went out a couple times, but that doesn't mean I want to marry her. And don't tell me you agree with Sam's matchmaking."

"I think Daddy's the last person in the world who should be matchmaking." Rome hesitated.

"But that doesn't mean I wouldn't like to see you find someone to share your life with. Marrying Cloe is the best thing that ever happened to me. You can't blame me for wanting the same for my little brother."

"I'm not like you, Rome. You've always been levelheaded, dependable, and responsible. All traits of a good husband." He glanced at the cradle. "And father. But we both know I got Mama's unreliability and irresponsibility. I think she proved those aren't good traits for a lasting relationship . . . or for a parent."

Rome studied him. "You're wrong, Casey. You might be a little more carefree than I am, but that doesn't mean you aren't responsible and dependable. I know I can always count on you when I need to. I think you'd make a great husband and father." He hesitated. "You just need to stop running scared."

"Running scared?"

He sighed. "I always thought Mama leaving hurt me more because I was old enough to remember her. But Cloe pointed out that just because you were too young to remember the time she spent here that doesn't mean her desertion hurt you less. Or screwed you up less. Her leaving made me not trust love. While I was willing to marry to make Daddy happy, I never believed that true love existed until I married Cloe. With you, I think Mama's leaving made you scared to commit to any woman—scared to love and not have that love returned."

"It sounds like you and Cloe have been psychoanalyzing me."

Rome shrugged. "We're both just worried about you."

"Well, there's no need to worry. I'm not running scared. I just don't want what you want, Rome. Now if you'll excuse me, I'm going to shower and head out to the Hellhole to be the irresponsible younger brother I am."

Rome placed a hand on his shoulder. "A younger brother I happen to love and just want the best for. If dating every woman in Wilder makes you happy, then I'll keep my mouth shut. But you're not heading out carousing until you've eaten dinner. Cloe made chicken potpie to thank you for the cradle and you'll stay and eat every speck of it."

Casey didn't argue. He might not like taking orders from his daddy, but he'd never minded taking orders from his brother. That, and he wasn't about to hurt Cloe's feelings.

It turned out she hadn't just made his favorite potpies. She'd also made one of his favorite desserts—a fudgy brownie with vanilla ice cream and chocolate syrup. Since she'd gone to all the trouble, he volunteered to do the dishes. By the time he was finished, it was well past nine o'clock and he still needed to shower and get ready.

Suddenly, driving all the way into town didn't sound all that appealing.

Especially if things weren't hopping at the Hellhole.

Pulling out his cellphone, he fired off a text to

his friend, Robby, who loved to party as much as he did and would no doubt be at the bar tonight.

You at Hellhole? How are things looking?

Robby answered immediately. Just not with what Casey expected.

Why didn't you tell me you were secretly fooling around with Noelle Holiday?

Casey's eyes widened. Mrs. Stokes! He had thought the old woman wasn't the type to gossip, but obviously he'd been wrong. He quickly replied.

You can't believe townsfolk's gossip. I'm not secretly fooling around with Noelle.

That's not how it looked in the video.

Casey stared at the text for a moment before replying. You saw the video?

Robby's reply arrived with a ping. Everyone has seen it. It's all over social media. Y'all are the talk of the Hellhole. What the hell's goin on?"

It was a good question.

He ignored Robby's text and instead tapped the app store open on his phone. Unlike most people, he didn't have social media accounts. He thought people posting every picture and video they took of their life was just plain stupid. Not to mention, they could be misinterpreted. Look at what had happened with Noelle's live post.

Casey preferred his life to remain private.

But it looked like it wasn't private now.

As soon as he had opened a social media account, he searched Noelle's name. A long line of reposted posts from a variety of different people popped up. Every post was of the video Noelle said she'd taken down. With those posts were all kinds of hashtags, mostly #thecowboyandthebaker #allIwantforchristmasisacowboyhero #bakinguploveintheholidaykitchen

The last hashtag caught his attention and he quickly searched *Holiday Kitchen*. A profile picture of Noelle in a white chef's hat popped up, along with all her posts. He scrolled through them, but didn't find the video he was looking for. Obviously, she *had* taken it down. She couldn't be blamed if people had reposted it. A lot of people. Hopefully, she had set them straight in her later posts.

He clicked on the most recent video and Noelle came to life. Her dark hair fell in soft wispy layers around her face, highlighting her wide green eyes and pouting lips—lips that, as usual, were painted a cherry red and moving a mile a minute.

"Hey, y'all! I promised you the best pumpkin pie recipe for your Thanksgiving feast and I'm here tonight to give it to you. Noelle's Great Pumpkin Pie is going to knock your socks off and all of your Thanksgiving guests' too. So let's get started with the piecrust we made the other night."

She adjusted the camera so it was focused on the marble countertop and the large disk of flour-coated dough. She started rolling the disk out. He knew she'd graduated from culinary school, but he'd never seen her bake before. It was mesmerizing. Using only the flats of her hands, she expertly rolled the long wooden pin. Her red-painted, close-cropped nails looked like pretty holly berries against the pale yellow piecrust. As she rolled she talked about everything from her two sisters getting ready to have babies to catching her daddy and mama kissing in the kitchen.

Once the piecrust was rolled into a large thin circle, she changed to a different topic. "And I guess I should tell you about the sweet gift I received today." One hand disappeared and then reappeared holding a big bouquet of red roses. "Aren't they stunning?"

Casey stared at his phone. Roses? Who would bring her roses? Had Noelle gotten back together with her ex? It made sense. You only gave a girl red roses when things were serious. Casey hadn't bought red roses in his life and probably never would.

"It was just so sweet it brought tears to my eyes," she continued. "I'm sure y'all know what I'm talking about—the kind of emotion that just grips your heart and gives it a tug."

Casey rolled his eyes, but her followers seemed to love it. The post had over ten thousand likes and close to two thousand comments that were filled with heart-eyed emojis. He couldn't help feeling stunned. He hadn't realized the *Holiday Kitchen* was so popular. No wonder the video had gone viral.

"It meant even more since we don't have a floral shop here in Wilder and he had to drive all the way to Austin to get them."

Now, Casey was completely confused. Why was she acting like her boyfriend lived in Wilder? Was she just ad-libbing? If she was, she needed to back off. Everyone knew everyone else in Wilder and the townsfolk who followed her were sure to call her out on the lie.

"And you know what he said when he gave them to me?" She made this fancy ruffle on the piecrust's edges using her fingers and thumb. When she finished, she wiped her hands with a towel before turning the camera back to her face. A face that was holding the dopiest look he had ever seen in his life. Her voice quivered with emotion as she finally got around to answering her own question.

"Ellie, you're the rose of my heart and I'll always be around to catch you when you fall . . . just like I did the other day when you were decorating and fell off the ladder."

Chapter Five

NOELLE LOVED WAKING up on Thanksgiving morning almost as much as she loved waking up on Christmas morning. The family farmhouse was always filled with the tempting aroma of roasting turkey and her mama's fresh-baked cinnamon rolls.

Her mama made cinnamon rolls every Thanksgiving and Christmas morning. Mostly because she didn't have time to cook her usual big breakfast because she was already busy making the holiday feast they would eat later. This year, there would be an even bigger feast with five new family members—six if you included Corbin's sister. And how could anyone not include Sunny Whitlock? She was like a bright ray of sunshine that filled any room with laughter and light.

Like the rest of her family, Noelle had fallen in love with Sunny at first sight and was thrilled she had accepted Mimi's invitation to stay at the ranch for Thanksgiving. But since Noelle had gotten home so late last night from Nothin' But Muffins, she hadn't had a chance to see Sunny. Something she intended to remedy this morning.

Jumping out of bed, she made her way to Cloe and Sweetie's old room, breathing in the wonderful scents of the holiday as she padded down the hallway in her snowman flannel pajamas.

She tapped on the door lightly before she eased it open. Sunny was sprawled face down on one of the twin beds like a starfish, her long arms and legs dangling off the too-small bed and all the blankets on the floor. A thick mass of long hair covered her face, loud snores emanating from the strawberry-blond waves.

Noelle had heard people snore before. Her daddy snored louder than a hibernating bear. But not even Daddy's snore could compare to Sunny's. Noelle stifled her laughter with her hand and started to pull the door closed. Before she could, Jelly Roll, Hallie and Jace's mangy black cat, streaked into the room and jumped on the bed—or more like Sunny's butt. The snoring stopped and Sunny sprang up, sending Jelly sailing.

Luckily, cats were good at landing on their feet.

"Wh-h-at!" Sunny pushed her hair out of her face and glanced around in confusion. When she spotted Noelle standing in the doorway, her big brown eyes widened before she released an excited gasp. "Is this another Secret Sisterhood initiation? What do I have to do? Race through the halls singing 'Yellow Rose of Texas'? Muck out the horse stalls in my pajamas? Not talk all through Thanksgiving dinner?"

Ever since the Holiday sisters had invited Sunny into their secret sisterhood club, she had been dying to prove herself worthy of the invitation. When the sisters had informed her the club didn't have any initiation rituals, besides skinny-dipping at Cooper Springs on a full moon, Sunny had looked so disappointed that Noelle and her sisters had agreed to give Sunny the occasional initiation dare just to make her happy.

As she stepped into the room, Noelle scooped up a disgruntled Jelly and considered Sunny's suggestions. Since Hallie had been looking forward to sleeping in with Jace this morning, she wouldn't appreciate Sunny running through the halls singing at the top of her lungs. And Noelle would never ask any woman to muck out stalls in their pajamas—especially if they were cute designer satin ones like Sunny wore. And no one at the Thanksgiving table would be happy if Sunny was silent. She was too entertaining.

But...it might be fun if someone else, someone who shouldn't even be invited to Thanksgiving dinner, was punished by the dare.

Noelle sat down on the opposite bed and smiled evilly. "Whenever someone says *turkey* today, you have to sock the person closest to you in the arm."

Sunny stared at her intently as if she'd just been given the *Mission Impossible* briefs that would explode at any second. "What if I have two people sitting on either side of me? And how hard do I sock them?"

"You can choose either one to sock and as hard as you want."

"But what if it's Mimi or Darla, there's no way

I can hit them. Or Sweetie or Cloe when they're pregnant. And if I sock Hallie, she'll knock me out."

"Then I'd choose to avoid them and try to sit next to someone at dinner who can take it." She knew exactly the womanizer who would rush to sit next to Sunny. Not that Sunny would mind. She had made it clear she was interested in Casey. Which meant Noelle needed to talk to her now before she saw the video and thought Noelle had broken the Secret Sisterhood rule of not poaching on another sister's man.

Noelle stroked Jelly's ratty fur. "There's something I need to talk to you about, Sunny."

Sunny got an excited look. "Is there an addendum to the dare? Whatever it is, I'll do it."

"No. This has to do with a freaky thing that happened the other night when I was videotaping my post for *Holiday Kitchen*."

"Oh, you mean Casey showing up and rescuing you." Sunny sighed. "If that wasn't the most romantic thing in the world, I don't know what is."

Noelle stared at her. "You follow me?"

"Of course I follow you. Don't all your sisters follow you?"

"No. My sisters rarely have time for social media now that they're married." Which in this case was probably a good thing.

"Well, I wouldn't hold it against them. They have been kind of busy getting married and preparing for babies." Sunny never held anything against anyone. It looked like she wasn't even going to hold a grudge against Noelle for taking a man she was interested in. Her smile was bright and her big brown eyes danced with deviltry as she joined Noelle on the bed. "So tell me all the juicy details. When did you two start secretly meeting? And is he a good lover?" Noelle's face heated, which made Sunny giggle with delight and bounce up and down, causing Jelly to jump off Noelle's lap and leave the room. "I knew it! The man looks like he knows his way around a bed."

Noelle shook her head. "I haven't been to bed with Casey and I have no desire to go there." She didn't know why an image popped into her head of her straddling him on the floor of Nothin' But Muffins. With that image came the memory of how it felt to have all those hard muscles pressed against her.

It had felt good. Extremely good.

Which was wrong. All wrong.

A chuckle pulled her from her thoughts. Sunny watched her with a knowing look in her eyes. "You sure about that?"

"I'm positive."

"Then why are you dating him?"

Noelle sighed. "I'm not."

Sunny stared at her with confusion. "I don't understand. You said yourself on your last post that you two are dating. He brought you gorgeous red roses. Why would he do that if you're not dating?"

Noelle released a frustrated huff as she flopped

back on the bed. "It was all a lie. He didn't bring me roses. I bought them for myself."

"What? Why?"

"Because I'm an egotistical idiot who is addicted to social media likes. Casey being my cowboy hero was all a mistake—something I planned to explain to my followers. But then I started getting all these likes and follows. The more I talked about Casey, the more likes and follows I got. And now I've dug a hole so deep I can't seem to dig my way out."

Sunny lay down next to her and stared up at the ceiling. Noelle expected disbelief and judgment. She should have known better. Sunny wasn't one to point fingers.

"I can see how that could happen. Everyone loves to be liked."

"Not so much that they'd perpetuate a lie."

"I don't know about that. I think there are a lot of people who would do just about anything for one of their posts to go viral. People use their spouses, pets, kids, and random people on the street to stage all kinds of things to get social media followers and likes. Even the people who aren't doing that, only show what they want people to see. And that's pretty much a form of lying. So you shouldn't feel too badly."

Noelle turned her head to look at her. "How did you get to be so nice?"

Sunny shrugged. "I'm not that nice. You should see me when I lose my temper."

"What? Do you stomp your foot and call someone a poopyhead?"

Sunny laughed. "Something like that. So tell me exactly what happened."

Noelle told Sunny everything about Casey showing up when she was filming and about discovering she'd gone viral and deciding to perpetuate the lie that she and Casey were dating. When she was finished, she rolled to her side to face Sunny.

"But I want you to know that it's all a hoax and I would never break the Secret Sisterhood oath of trespassing on another sister's man. I know you like Casey and, believe me, he's all yours."

Sunny didn't look relieved. In fact, she looked more than a little disappointed. But maybe it was just a trick of the sunlight pouring in through the window. Because a second later, the look was replaced with a big smile. "Nice to know. So how long is this hoax going to continue? And does Casey know about it?"

"He knows about the video, but he doesn't know that I'm pretending we're still in a relationship."

"And you're not going to tell him, I take it."

"There's no need to. The only people who would know it was Casey who rescued me the other night are the townsfolk and, like Casey, most of them aren't even on social media. The ones that are know Casey and I are like kerosene and a lit match. So once I implement my plan—" A plan she'd been up all night concocting. "They'll just think they misunderstood what was going on that night."

"You've lost me," Sunny said. "What plan?"

Noelle smiled. "I plan to give my followers exactly what they want—the baker and the hot cowboy."

"And how do you plan to do that without Casey?"

Noelle smiled. "Casey isn't the only tall, hot cowboy in Wilder."

―

The rest of the morning flew by as Noelle helped her mama get everything ready for dinner. Due to *Holiday Kitchen* posts, the pies were baked and lined up on the counter waiting to be sliced and complemented with big scoops of homemade whipped or ice cream. But there were still dinner rolls to make and all the sides that went with the two turkeys roasting in the ovens and the ham simmering in Dr Pepper in the Crock-Pot.

Usually, they ate Thanksgiving dinner at the big kitchen table. But this year, with their enlarged family, they needed much more seating. So it was decided—mostly by Liberty and Belle, the family event planners—that everyone would eat in the barn.

Noelle had to hand it to the twins. They did a great job of decorating. The night before, they had set up portable banquet tables to make one long dining table and then covered it in white linen. They hung over thirty mason jars with tea light candles on a wire they had their husbands string from the rafters over the table. More mason jars were filled with wildflowers and used as centerpieces. Once the great-grandmas' china, silverware, and crystal glasses were placed on the table, it looked like it belonged in a country lifestyle magazine.

Although the real credit for making the setting perfect went to Daddy, Hallie, Jace, Corbin, and Jesse who had released all the horses into the paddock early that morning and cleaned out the stalls so the barn smelled like fresh hay rather than fresh horse poop.

Once the table was set and most of the food prepared, Noelle slipped upstairs to shower and get ready. She chose her favorite dress printed with bunches of cherries hanging from green stems. Not only was it cute and stylish, but also the high waistline gave her tummy plenty of space for extra pie and dinner rolls. The shorter hem showed just enough leg to catch the attention of a certain assistant ranch manager without being too inappropriate for a family gathering.

She had been thrilled when Mimi had told her Reid Mitchell and his niece, Sophie, would be coming to Thanksgiving dinner. Reid was the perfect cowboy to take Casey's place on her social media platform. He even owned a black Stetson. It would be easy to just exchange one cowboy for another. And now that she thought about it, maybe fate had set up the entire fiasco with Casey just so she would end up with Reid.

A hard rap on the door startled her. Assuming it was one of her sisters, she finished tugging on a red cowboy boot as she yelled for them to come in.

But it wasn't one of her sisters who stepped into the room.

It was the cowboy she wanted to exchange.

Except Casey didn't look like the cocky, carefree man she knew and hated. His signature black Stetson was missing and his hair looked like a windswept wheat field. Gone was the annoying smirk and in its place was a stern frown. His eyes weren't twinkling teasingly. In fact, they were dark and intense as they pinned her.

Suddenly, all the oxygen seemed to be sucked out of the room and Noelle struggled to catch her breath as he spoke in a deep, growly voice she'd never heard before.

"You said you were going to take the video down. Not turn me into your fake, rose-delivering boyfriend."

Crap. He knew.

She grabbed her other boot and tried to bluff her way through. "I don't know what you think you're doing, Casey Remington, but you can't just barge into a woman's bedroom."

"I didn't barge. I knocked and you invited me in."

"Because I didn't know it was you."

He stepped closer to the bed, and when she finished tugging on the other boot and straightened, her gaze was level with the part of his anatomy she'd been struggling to forget. The fly of his jeans wasn't as bulging as it had been the other day, but it still made her feel like she had been tossed in a preheated five-hundred-degree oven.

He placed those work-calloused hands on his

hips as if showcasing his virility. "Who did you think it was? Your hot cowboy hero?"

She pulled her gaze away from his fly and lifted her gaze to his eyes. He was mad. Spitting mad. She had never seen him like this before. While she was always ticked off at him, he had never been ticked off at her. There was something about their reversed roles that caused her world to tip on its axis. She could deal with teasing, smug Casey. She didn't know how to deal with angry, intense Casey. And not because she feared him. Fear had nothing to do with her breath getting hung up in her lungs or the tingling heat that settled low in her belly.

"So?" he said, taking a step closer until his jeans brushed her knees. "Are you going to explain?"

She stood, hoping that would help her get control of whatever was happening to her body. But that only put her closer to another tempting part of his. His lips. Lips that she had only seen curved in a teasing smirk. Never pressed in an angry line that highlighted a tiny scar. She had never noticed the scar before, and the sight of it cutting into the top curve of his lip make her feel even more unbalanced.

"What happened to your lip?"

Those lips parted in a surprised huff. "As if you don't remember throwing that pencil with deadly aim in fifth grade." She did remember throwing the pencil at him for something mean he'd said to her, but she hadn't thought she'd scarred him. He'd walked away laughing . . . and obviously bleeding. "And don't think you can change the subject." He gripped her arms, not roughly, but with just enough pressure to make her extremely aware of his strength. "I want an explanation, Ellie. And I want it now."

The commanding tone made her feel even more strange and breathless. But before she could figure out what in the world was going on with her, Sunny walked in.

"Hey, Elle—oh, sorry, I didn't mean to interrupt."

Whatever weird spell Angry Casey had cast over her broke and Noelle jerked away from him.

"You're not interrupting. Casey was just—"

"Lost." He flashed Sunny a charming smile, all anger gone. "Would you be so kind as to point me in the right direction of the bathroom, Sunny?"

Sunny glanced at Noelle in question before she nodded. "Of course. I'm an expert at showing people the way." She turned to leave and Casey followed. But before he stepped out of the room, he glanced back at Noelle, his fiery blue eyes branding her with their intensity.

"This isn't finished, Ellie."

Chapter Six

IT WAS STRANGE being part of a big family Thanksgiving. All the Thanksgivings Casey could remember had been shared with only his brother and father. After Mama left, Sam had hired a woman to take care of him and Rome. Mabel had also cleaned house and cooked, including their holiday meals. But when Casey was in fourth grade, she'd retired and moved to Houston to be near her grandkids and Sam decided his sons were old enough to fend for themselves.

For a few Thanksgivings and Christmases, Sam bought a turkey last minute and attempted to cook it. It hadn't gone well. Either he forgot to thaw it out and it was half raw when he took it out of the oven or he cooked it to the consistency of saddle leather. He finally gave up and started ordering a smoked turkey from the Hellhole.

But those smoked turkeys looked nothing like the turkeys that graced the mile-long table in the Holidays' barn. Casey's mouth watered at just the sight of the crispy golden-skinned birds that were surrounded by more side dishes than he had seen in his life.

Bowls of whipped potatoes, creamed corn, and cranberry sauce. Casserole dishes of candied yams, cornbread stuffing, and green beans covered in fried onions. Platters of fresh veggies with ranch, pitchers of rich gravy, a huge glistening ham studded with cloves, and baskets of fluffy dinner rolls. It was like Casey had died and gone to food heaven . . . or it would be if not for the devil in the short cherry dress who was flitting around taking pictures of the table before everyone took their seats. No doubt, those pictures would end up on the *Holiday Kitchen* social media page, accompanied with more lies about her cowboy hero boyfriend.

The thought caused his anger to flare once again. He couldn't remember ever feeling this mad. Not even at his father. He wasn't the angry Remington. He was the happy one. But as he watched Noelle, he didn't feel happy. Not happy at all.

"So you want to explain why the normally charming Casey Remington has turned into the Grinch before he has the 'wonderful, awful idea?'"

Casey turned to Sunny. She looked stunning as usual in skinny jeans and a sweater that showed off her tall, slender figure. If her two brothers, Corbin and Jesse, hadn't informed him that they'd skin him alive if he tried to date her, he would have already made a play for her.

Or maybe not.

He liked her too much.

"Wonderful, awful ideas are my specialties," he said with an evil grin.

She laughed. "I bet they are. But being mad at Elle isn't wonderful. It's just awful. From what she told me, she didn't mean for things to get so out of hand."

He stared at her. "She didn't mean it? She's the one acting like I'm some kind of cowboy Romeo who's madly in love with her."

Before Sunny could reply, Hallie's voice boomed. "For Pete's sake, Elle! Enough pictures already. People are hungry and the turkey's getting cold."

"Turkey," Sunny muttered before she turned to Casey and socked him in the arm.

He was stunned. Sunny wouldn't hurt a fly. "What was that for?"

She smiled brightly. "Haven't you ever heard it's lucky to get punched by a friend on Thanksgiving?"

He rubbed his arm. "No."

"Well, now you have. Let's eat!" He started to follow her to the table, but she turned to him and shook her head. "You need to sit with Noelle and get all that pent-up anger out before it turns into a grudge." She winked at him. "You wouldn't want to end up like my brother, now would you?"

She had a good point. A grudge was how Corbin had ended up married to Belle. Not that anything would get Casey to marry Noelle. But if he wanted to enjoy this heavenly feast, he needed to get over his anger and go back to the happy-go-lucky guy he was. The only way he could do that was to convince Noelle to clear things up on her social media feed.

He headed to the empty chair next to her, but when he started to pull it out, she grabbed it and held firm. "Reid Mitchell is sitting here."

Casey glanced at the assistant ranch manager who was talking with Hank Holiday. All the women in town were gossiping about how good-looking Reid was. The gossip hadn't bothered Casey at all. Until now. For some strange reason, the thought that Noelle had been saving Reid a seat did not sit well. Casey tugged the chair free from her grip with a little more force than was necessary before he sat down.

"Now, I'm sure Reid would rather sit with his niece. You don't want to separate a family on Thanksgiving, do you, Ellie? Especially when we have so much to talk about."

She glared at him. "We have nothing to say to each other."

"You might not have anything to say to me, but I have plenty to say to you." But once everyone was seated at the table, he realized there was no way he could say what he wanted. She realized it too. The smile she sent him was smug and annoying.

"So what did you want to say, Case?" She glanced at her daddy who sat at the head of the table and her mama who sat directly across from them. "I'm sure everyone would love to hear it."

He looked at her parents and pinned on a smile. "I just want to say how grateful I am to be invited to this bountiful feast."

Darla beamed. "You're more than welcome, Casey. You're part of our family now and we couldn't be more thrilled to have you." She glanced at Hank and Noelle. "Isn't that right?"

They gave identical snorts before Mimi, who sat between Darla and Sunny, spoke. "Of course we're thrilled. We now have everyone we need to make this ranch what it's destined to be. Now let's bow our heads so we can give thanks before we dig into that turkey."

"Turkey," Sunny repeated. She turned to Reid Whitlock who had taken a seat on her right and socked him in the arm.

The meal was better than any meal Casey had ever had in his life. Since he couldn't yell at Noelle like he wanted to, he focused on every delightful bite. He devoured his first helping and then went for seconds. He was savoring the gravy-drenched dressing when he glanced over and noticed Noelle watching him.

He swallowed the bite. "What?"

Her gaze lowered to his mouth. Thinking he had something on it, he lifted his napkin and wiped it off. But her long, dark lashes remained lowered. Her lips parted as if she was going to say something, but nothing came out. Even after eating and drinking, that cupid bow mouth was still the color of the cherries on her dress. Although the color wasn't as shiny as it had been. As if she'd read his thoughts, her tongue swept out and wet her lips.

Just like that, heat washed through Casey like a late summer flash flood and the fork he still held slipped from his fingers and clattered to his plate, causing everyone at their end of the table to look at him.

"Pardon me," he said. When everyone had gone back to their meals and conversations, he glanced at Noelle, expecting to find her smirking. But she wasn't. Instead, she was looking down at her plate with her cheeks flaming.

Casey didn't know what had just happened. All he knew was that he didn't want it to happen again. Which meant he needed to get things settled with Noelle.

He leaned in closer and whispered next to her ear, "Meet me behind the barn."

She shivered as if she were cold. The barn was a little chilly. Which didn't explain why he felt so overheated as he breathed in the scent of baked cookies that seemed to seep from her pores.

"I have no intentions of meeting you anywhere," Noelle said without looking at him.

"So you want me to talk about the video in front of your parents? Because I will. I'm sure they'll love to hear about their daughter's deception."

"Fine." She tossed her napkin onto her plate and scooted back her chair.

As she headed out of the barn, he glanced across the table and saw Mimi and Sunny watching her. Once she was gone, they leaned their heads together and started whispering. They stopped whispering when they noticed him watching. They both drew apart and pinned on innocent smiles, but it was obvious the two women were up to something. He just didn't have time to figure out what. He had his own problems to deal with.

He waited a few minutes before he excused himself and followed Noelle. When he came around the barn, he found her sitting on the seat of an old tractor. In the cherry dress and red cowboy boots with the light autumn breeze fluttering her dark hair, she made the perfect picture of a country girl.

Although the scowl didn't quite go with the image.

"You've got five minutes to yell and get all your anger out."

He moved closer, dried leaves crackling under his boots. "Five minutes isn't gonna do it. I'm not sure five days would. What are you thinking acting like I'm madly in love with you?"

"I haven't been acting like you're madly in love with me. I've been acting like the cowboy in the video was madly in love with me."

His eyes widened. "I am the cowboy in the video!"

She glanced over her shoulder at the barn. "Would you lower your voice? I know you're the cowboy, but none of my other followers do."

"I don't care about some random followers. I care about the entire town thinking I've fallen for you."

"And why is that, Case? Are you worried that all the women you convinced you don't do love will show up at your door with pitchforks?"

That was exactly what he was worried about. "I

don't do love and I don't want some social media diva who just wants followers and likes convincing people that I do."

He thought she was going to keep arguing, Noelle had always been stubborn as a mule, but she surprised him.

She blew out her breath in a long huff. "You're right. I did let things get a little carried away."

"A little?"

"Fine. A lot. I only planned to play along with vague references to the video, but things just sort of snowballed."

"Are you sure about that? Or was this all a plan to get back at me for all the teasing I've done to you over the years."

Those cherry lips parted to reveal a brilliant flash of teeth. "Maybe. Although there's nothing I can do to get back at you for all the things you did to me, Casey Remington."

"Besides a little harmless teasing, I haven't done anything to you."

"Harmless?" Her smile faded and she jumped down from the tractor right in front of him. "Stealing the dessert from my lunchbox almost every day wasn't harmless teasing. Neither was slipping that horny toad into the pocket of my coat so I screamed and embarrassed myself—not to mention my entire family—in church. Neither was setting off those firecrackers during my Miss Soybean speech so I ended up losing. And using a horrible nickname is not harmless teasing. Especially when it was you who farted in class and blamed it on me!"

"Those were just childish pranks. And Smelly Ellie was all in fun."

"Maybe when we were in elementary school, but not when I was an impressible teenager with low self-esteem."

"Low self-esteem? You've never had low self-esteem in your life, Ellie. You've always thought you were God's gift to the world. Which is why you have no problem jumping on social media and telling folks your entire life story. And that's fine as long as you don't include me in your story."

She rose up on the toes of her boots, bringing those red-hot lips inches from his. "Oh, let's talk about people who think they're God's gift to the world, shall we? You have thought you walked on water ever since we were kids. And every woman in this town has supported your belief. Which is why you're so upset. You're worried they'll stop thinking it if you get a steady girlfriend. Well, grow up, Case. A steady girlfriend isn't going to cramp your style. In fact, it might just help it. Women will like you better if they think there's actually a possibility you can commit instead of being a womanizing man whore."

He'd been so proud of himself for keeping his anger under control. But damn if this woman didn't have a way of lighting his fuse. "I'm not a womanizing man whore!"

"Really? What would you call it?"

"A man who just isn't ready to settle down. And I never lie about it. I make that clear to every woman I date."

She lifted her eyebrows. "Date? I wouldn't call

buying them a couple shots of tequila before you take them to bed a date, Case."

"Obviously, you know nothing about my dates. I don't think one woman I've taken out will complain."

"I think you're wrong. I think they complain plenty when they wake up the following morning and you're gone."

"And I guess you think it's better to lead men on and then dump them?"

Her eyes flashed with green fire and he couldn't help feeling happy that he'd made her as angry as she made him. "I don't lead men on!"

"What would you call your serial dating? How many men have you made believe they are the one, Ellie—the mythical man who is going to fulfill all your dreams and be gifted the elusive blossom?"

She slapped him so hard his ears rang before she turned and headed around the side of the barn. He ran and caught up with her, taking her arm and pulling her around to face him. He expected to see her green eyes flashing with anger. He did not expect to see them glittering with tears. The sight caused all the anger to drain right out of him.

"Elle. I'm sorry. I didn't mean to make you cry."

"That's such bullshit. You love to make me cry. You've always loved to make me cry." She jerked away from him. "Who told you?"

He sighed and ran a hand through his hair. "You know how people love to gossip about everything in this town."

Her eyes widened. "People have been talking about my virginity?"

He stared at her. "What? I was talking about all the men you've dated. Why would you think I was talking about . . . wait a second. You're still a virgin?"

Her cheeks flushed almost as red as her lips and he felt like she'd slapped him all over again. "If you don't know what it means, then why did you use the term *my elusive blossom*?"

"Because, when we were in seventh grade, you kept yelling 'You'll never get my blossom, Casey Remington!' every time I teased you. I just assumed it was your love."

"Why would you think I was talking about love?"

"Because who calls their virginity their blossom?"

Her face got even redder and she pointed a finger at him. "I swear if you tell a single soul . . ."

"You'll what? Make everyone think I'm madly in love with you on social media?"

"Fine! If you keep your mouth shut, I'll convince everyone you're not my cowboy hero."

"And how are you going to do that when the video has already trended?"

She lifted her chin. "I'm going to swap you out for a much nicer cowboy. One who doesn't have commitment issues." Before he could ask what she meant, she turned and walked away.

He stood there for a moment, still reeling over the fact that Noelle was a virgin. It made absolutely no sense. The woman might not be his type, but he couldn't deny she had the kind of soft, full-figured body that would tempt a saint. Which probably explained why Casey's mind had gone off the Noelle-is-not-my-type tracks lately. And not one of the men she had dated had tried to get her into bed?

Of course, maybe they had tried, but just not succeeded.

Why did that suddenly feel like a challenge?

Absolutely not, Casey Remington.

He shoved the crazy thought out of his head with a bulldozer.

Noelle's blossom was completely off limits.

Chapter Seven

"Well, that's what a Thanksgiving should be." Mimi took a sip of her homemade elderberry wine. If her twinkling eyes were any indication, it wasn't her first glass of the day. Nor was it Daddy's. Hank didn't care for large gatherings, but he seemed pretty pleased at the moment.

"You're right, Mama," he said as he held his glass of wine up and toasted his wife who was cuddled on the swing next to him. "To the best Thanksgiving ever!"

Mama took a sip of her wine and smiled softly. "It was a wonderful day, wasn't it?"

"Perfect." Hallie rested her head on Jace's shoulder and smiled up at him as he stroked the fat cat sitting on his lap.

"The best." Sunny clinked her glass against the one Noelle held. "Wasn't it, Elle?"

Noelle tried her best to smile as she nodded, but it hadn't been the best day for her.

Once again, Casey Remington had ruined things for her. She hadn't even been able to enjoy one bite of food with him sitting so close. If he hadn't invaded her space with his manly scent and brushes of his knee or broad shoulders, he'd distracted her with the moans and mmm's he made every time he took a bite of food. She knew he'd done it on purpose. He had always loved ruining things for her.

And now he knew she was a virgin.

She didn't doubt for a second he would use the knowledge against her if she didn't make it clear on social media he wasn't the cowboy hero who was madly in love with her. The only way to do that was to start dating Reid and get him to do a post with her. One cowboy in a Stetson was as good as another. Even if Reid didn't want to date her, maybe he'd be nice enough to play along just until her new followers were hooked on her baking posts. He seemed like a nice guy.

Unlike Casey.

She set down her glass of wine. "Well, I think I'm going to walk off all the turkey I consumed." She cringed when she realized what she'd said. Especially since she was sitting next to Sunny.

Sunny sent her an apologetic look before she slugged her in the arm. "I'll go with you."

"No, you stay here and enjoy the rest of your wine." The hurt expression on Sunny's face had Noelle leaning in to whisper, "I'm going to see Reid."

"Are you sure that's a good idea?" Sunny whispered back. "I mean . . . Reid seems a little grumpy to me."

"That could be because you punched him all through dinner."

"What was I supposed to do? Punch Mimi?"

Mimi must have heard her name. "What are you two whispering about over there?"

"Nothin'!" they chimed together.

The walk to Cooper Springs didn't take any time at all. The large spring-fed pool of water was surrounded by a copse of oaks and cypress trees. Corbin and Belle were building a house on the other side of those trees and Reid had parked his old trailer on this side, just to the left of the path leading from the Holiday house.

According to Hallie, Reid and Sophie were just planning on living in the trailer until Reid could find a place in town. Noelle hoped that was soon. The little hitch trailer looked too cramped for one person, let alone two, sitting amid the trees with its tiny windows glowing in the dark night.

Holding the pumpkin pie she'd brought in one hand, Noelle knocked on the tiny door. Only a few seconds later, it was pulled open by Sophie. She was a pretty teenager with shoulder-length dark brown hair and hazel eyes the same whiskey shade as her uncle's. But like most teenage girls, she seemed to be struggling with how much makeup to wear. She'd showed up for Thanksgiving dinner looking like a Broadway stage actress. Now, most of that makeup was under her eyes, giving her the appearance of a demon child straight from hell.

Her greeting was just as friendly.

"Oh. It's you."

Noelle pinned on a smile. "Hey, Sophie!" She

held up the pie. "I thought y'all would like some leftover pumpkin pie."

"I don't like pumpkin—"

Reid appeared behind his niece. He looked a little disheveled, but still hot as sin with his messed black hair and half-snapped western shirt. "That's real nice of you, Miss Noelle."

She shrugged. "Just being neighborly."

Sophie crossed her arms and glared down at Noelle through the screen door. "Sure you are."

"Watch your manners, Soph," Reid scolded before he moved his niece out of the way and held open the door. "Would you like to come in?" He glanced over his shoulder and frowned. "Or maybe it would be better if I came out. Things are a little cramped in here." Without touching the metal steps, his long legs easily covered the space from the trailer to the ground. He moved over to the two folding camping chairs set up under a raggedy striped awning. "Please have a seat. Can I get you something to drink? I think we have bottled water, Gatorade, and Dr Pepper."

"No, thank you. I'm good. Like I said, I just stopped by to bring you some pie." She glanced down at the pie tin in her hands. "Obviously, I should have brought apple. I didn't realize you didn't like pumpkin."

"I like pumpkin just fine." He took the pie tin from her and set it on a lopsided table before gesturing at one of the chairs. "Are you sure you won't sit and stay awhile?"

"Well, maybe just a little while." She sat down and he followed suit, taking the other chair. There was a long, awkward silence before she stumbled on a conversation starter. "So how do you like working on the ranch?"

"I like it just fine."

"I guess you've been cowboying for a long time."

"A while."

"I heard Sophie was the kicker on the high school football team."

"She was."

Noelle had never struggled to talk to a man in her life, but she was struggling now. She tried at least five more conversation starters, but not one received anything other than a few words. She was thinking about just coming right out and asking him on a date, when the screen door opened and Sophie popped her head out.

"Uncle Reid! Your cellphone's ringing. It's Hallie."

Reid hopped up. "Pardon me. I should get that."

Noelle got to her feet. "No problem. I need to get going anyway."

"Thanks again for the pie!" he called before he stepped inside. "Go get the pie, Soph, and be sure and say thank you."

Sophie pushed the screen door open so hard it slammed against the side of the trailer. Noelle took a step back as the scary-looking teenager thumped down the steps in baggy sweats and a pair of flip-flops.

"Thanks for the pie."

Noelle cleared her throat. "You're welcome. Next time, I'll bring you an apple pie."

Sophie's black-ringed eyes narrowed. "You think I don't know what you're doin'? In just the last week, six women have knocked on our door, bearing all kinds of foil or plastic wrapped food in the hopes of getting my uncle into bed."

Noelle should have known she wouldn't be the first woman in Wilder to come calling on the new hot cowboy. She now understood why Sophie was so belligerent. It had to be annoying having horny women constantly arriving at the door with baked goods.

"Well, I'm not hoping to get your uncle into bed." After what happened with Kenny, she didn't know if she would ever try to get a man into bed again.

"Then what *are* you hoping for? Because from what I've seen on social media, you already have a boyfriend."

Great. Even demon teenagers had seen the video. "Well, you can't believe everything you see on social media."

"So Casey's not your boyfriend?"

Before she could answer, headlights came bouncing toward them. Noelle didn't recognize Sunny's Subaru until it came to a dust-spitting stop in front of the trailer—after running over both camp chairs. Sunny hopped out at the same time as Reid came out of the trailer.

"What the hell?" he said.

Sunny looked down at the black metal leg of a crumpled chair hanging out from beneath the grille of her car. "Oops! Sorry." She glanced at Reid and shook her finger. "But that's no excuse for cussing in front of a minor. Teenage years are the most impressionable." She flashed a smile at Sophie. "Hello again. Love the smoky-eye look. I'd ask for a private tutorial, but I don't have time." Her gaze landed on Noelle. "We got to go. Your mama fell out of the swing and your Mimi thinks she broke her arm."

Noelle was instantly concerned. "Is she okay?"

"I just got off the phone from Hallie," Reid said. "She said your mama is fine."

"Drunk would be a better word," Sunny chimed in. "When they were getting in Jace's truck to head to the county hospital, she and your daddy were giggling like a couple of kids from all the elderberry wine they'd had. So I doubt she feels a thing. But we should get going. I told them that we'd meet them there."

Noelle said a quick goodbye to Reid and Sophie before getting into the passenger side of Sunny's Subaru. She barely got her seat belt fastened before Sunny popped the car into reverse and backed out in a plume of dust . . . and the crunch of camp chairs.

"I'll pay for those!" she yelled out the window as they took off.

When they finally hit paved road and weren't being jostled around like beans in a bag, Noelle turned to her. "So what happened? How did my mama fall out of the porch swing?"

"Oh, she didn't fall out of the porch swing. She fell out of the swing in the old oak tree. I guess your daddy was pushing her and pushed a little too hard."

Noelle rolled her eyes. "For the love of Pete. Those two have been acting like two lovesick teenagers lately."

"And what's wrong with that—I mean, besides a broken arm. I think it's sweet they're spicing things up after being married for so long." Sunny shot a glance over at her. "And speaking of spicing things up, how did your seduction of Reid go?"

"You sound like Sophie. I'm not trying to seduce Reid. I'm just trying to . . ." She struggled to find the right words and Sunny helped her out.

"Use him to fulfill your desire for social media likes."

Noelle slumped down in the seat and sighed. "Something like that. And before you give me a lecture, I've changed my mind. Not only because using a nice guy is the wrong thing to do, but also because no one would mistake Reid for Casey."

"You're right. They are night and day. One is as grumpy as my daddy after too many Bud Lights and the other is nice as pie."

"I'm assuming you think Casey is the pie," she said sarcastically.

"He's always been nice to me." Sunny glanced over at her. "I think he'd be nice to you too if you'd let him."

"If I'd let him?"

Sunny sent her a pointed look. "You bristle up like a porcupine whenever he's around, Elle. It's hard to be nice when you're dodging sharp quills."

"Because he's always doing something to make me mad—on purpose, I might add."

"Maybe he's not trying to make you mad. Maybe he's just trying to get your attention."

"Well, he certainly isn't happy about having my attention now. He's terrified my posts will change his image from a womanizing playboy who can't commit to a loving boyfriend who can."

Sunny laughed. "The man does have commitment issues. But most men do. At least Casey is up front about his." She hesitated. "Of course, all it takes is the love of a good woman to change all that. And maybe that's what has your followers so enthralled. Everyone loves a bad boy gone good."

"Maybe. But in this case, the bad boy has no intentions of going good."

Sunny smiled slyly. "Then maybe a good girl needs to go bad."

Chapter Eight

Nothin' But Muffins was dead the Friday after Thanksgiving. The parking spaces in front were all empty and not a soul sat at the tables Casey could see through the window. Either everyone in town had gone to the big cities to Christmas shop or they'd stuffed themselves on turkey and pumpkin pie and had no room for muffins.

Of course, Casey wasn't there for muffins either. He was there to make sure Noelle had cleared things up with her followers. He'd been checking her profile page all day, and so far, there hadn't been one post and he wanted to know what was taking so long. He was ready to wash his hands of this Noelle Holiday situation so things could go back to normal.

Because he sure didn't feel normal now.

He felt grumpy and jumpy and not anything like his easygoing self. And people were starting to take notice. Rome and Cloe kept asking him if everything was all right and, this morning, he caught Sam looking at him with concern. It *was* concerning. Casey was extremely concerned about all the thoughts that kept popping into his head. Thoughts that were all centered on an annoying baker with cherry-red lips. He wanted them to stop.

He parked his truck and hopped out. The temperature had dropped and it finally felt like fall had arrived. He flipped up the collar of his fleece-lined jean jacket as he moved through the brisk wind toward the door.

As soon as the bell jangled, Noelle appeared in the doorway of the kitchen. It was obvious she'd been baking. She had an oven mitt on one hand and flour dusted the ruffled holly apron she wore. Her welcoming smile fizzled as soon as she saw him.

"Oh. You."

"I guess you were hoping for Reid Mitchell."

Last night, his mind had gone back to what Noelle had said about finding a cowboy who knew how to commit. He'd realized that was why she'd saved a seat for Reid at Thanksgiving dinner. She wanted Reid as Casey's replacement. Her next words confirmed it.

"Reid would be a much more welcome sight."

His anger returned and he scowled. "Look, I don't care what cowboy you replace me with as long as you do."

She placed the mitt-covered hand on her hip and matched his scowl. "Is that why you're here? To make sure I let all your girlfriends know you're still available? Well, you don't need to worry. I plan on posting as soon as I close up."

"About your new boyfriend Reid?"

What the hell? Why couldn't he shut up about Reid? Of course, he knew why. Just the thought of Noelle giving Reid her blossom made him feel like hitting something. He didn't know why. He shouldn't care who she gave her blossom to. But for some reason he did. This was confirmed when he was flooded with relief at her next words.

"Reid isn't going to be my new cowboy hero. No one is. I'm just going to tell my followers that I'm heading back to Dallas after the holidays so I decided it doesn't make sense to get in a serious relationship. And I decided to break things off with you."

"That's not exactly coming clean. You were never with me."

She sent him an annoyed look. "I know that, but would it hurt you to just play along this once. You owe me for all the hell you've put me through over the years."

He figured she had a point. "Fine. Just as long as you make it clear that it's over between us." He hesitated. "So why Dallas? I mean it's a nice city, but you seem pretty happy to be back with your family and working here at Nothin' But Muffins."

She glanced around and smiled. "I do love working here. But once Sheryl gets back, I won't be needed. And I have to make a living doing something. I've applied at numerous hotels and restaurants in Dallas as a pastry chef. Hopefully, one will pan out."

"If those Thanksgiving pies you made are any

indication, I'm sure you'll have no problem getting a job."

She stared at him. "Was that a compliment, Casey Remington?"

He shrugged. "Just saying those were damn good pies."

"You would know. You tried every single one."

"What can I say? I have a sweet tooth."

She studied him intently for a second before she waved her mitt. "Come on back in the kitchen, I need your help."

"With what?"

"Taste-testing my new muffin."

He really wished he and his high school buddies hadn't used the word *muffin* to describe a certain female body part. Because her words instantly evoked a naughty image of Noelle sitting on the stainless-steel island wearing nothing but her ruffled apron with her legs spread invitingly.

"Case? Are you okay?"

It took a real effort to push the image out of his mind. "Yeah. I'm fine. I just . . . uhh . . . need to get back to the ranch. So I'll have to taste your . . . umm . . . muffin another time." Was his face on fire? He felt like his face was flaming from the inside out.

"Don't be silly. It won't take but a second. And take off your coat. You look like you're burning up." She whirled and headed back to the kitchen.

Casey should probably slip out the door. Plenty of work *did* await him back at the ranch. But for some reason, he didn't leave. Maybe it was the thought of going back out in the icy wind when the café was so warm and cozy with its glowing Christmas tree in the corner and the delicious scent filling the air. Or maybe it was the lure of Noelle's muffin. Whatever the reason, he took off his jacket and hung it on the coatrack before following her into the kitchen.

The delicious scent was even stronger in here. He took a deep breath as he watched her put on another mitt and pull two trays of steamy, plump muffins out of the oven.

"I have two contenders for a new holiday muffin," she said as she set them on the stainless-steel countertop. "The Sugarplum Fairy muffin and the Merry Berry muffin. For the Sugarplum Fairy, I used a batter similar to the flavors in a sugar cookie dough, but instead of vanilla, I used almond extract. I filled it with diced plums and added a sugared plum slice to the top. For the Merry Berry muffins, I used a batter similar to the one we use for our blueberry muffins, but instead of blueberries I added a raspberry compote swirl, then topped with three sugared raspberries. Which one do you want to—no wait, let me surprise you."

She tugged off her mitts, then took him by the arms and positioned him with his back against the counter. "Close your eyes."

"Close my eyes? I don't think so. Not when the rolling pin you threatened me with is sitting right there."

"Don't be silly. If I wanted to hit you in the head with a rolling pin, I would have done it the other night. And as much as I've dreamed about poisoning you, I'm not going to do it today. Now close your eyes."

He studied her for a moment before he did what she asked. Only a few seconds later, something warm and soft brushed his lips. He opened his mouth and a muffin was crammed in. It was good, but it was nothing compared to the next muffin she offered him. This muffin was warm and sugary and flavored with sweet little chunks of plum.

"Sweet Lord," he muttered around the confection. "This is awesome."

"Awesome how?"

He swallowed and opened his eyes. "Awesome as in that's the best thing I've ever tasted in my life."

Her entire face lit up like the Christmas tree in the other room. He couldn't ever remember making Noelle smile. It felt good. Damn good.

"I knew it!" She punched the air. "Sugarplum Fairy it is!" She peeled back the wrapper of the muffin she held and took a big bite and then closed her eyes as she chewed. "I knew this was the one. It's just . . . sinful delight."

What was sinful delight was the woman standing in front of him.

He'd always thought Noelle was pretty. But this close, he could see how creamy her complexion was and how delicate her features. She'd pulled her long bangs back with a stretchy red headband, revealing her high forehead and the arched perfection of her dark eyebrows. Thick twin fans of lashes rested on her high cheekbones and there was a smudge of flour on the tip of her button nose. But it was her cupid bow lips that held his attention. They were more of a dusty rose color today and dusted with crystalized sugar that glittered like tiny diamonds as she spoke.

"It's like sugar cookies and plum pudding mixed in one perfect little muffin package." She took another bite and moaned. The sound slammed into him like a Brahman bull at full speed. He wanted to hear that sound again . . . but this time, he wanted to be the cause of it.

Without any direction from his brain, he lowered his head and ran his tongue along her plump sugarcoated bottom lip. Her breath sucked in and her eyes flashed open. He braced for the slap that was sure to come. Or a crack over the head with her rolling pin. And he deserved it. What had he been thinking, licking Noelle like she was a big scoop of his favorite plum sherbet?

But she didn't slap him. Or crack him over the head.

Those bright green eyes stared back at him for only a second before she dropped what remained of the muffin, grabbed the front of his shirt . . . and tugged him closer.

Talk about sinful delight. Her lips were better than any muffin. They settled against his in a soft press before they opened and invited him into the wet heat of her mouth. Once he got a taste, he realized he'd made a big mistake. Noelle was the best thing he'd ever tasted in his life. And he wanted more. Much more. He wanted to gobble her up until there was nothing left.

She seemed to feel the same way.

She gripped his shirt so tightly it cut into the back of his neck. When he tried to change the angle of the kiss for a deeper fit, she fisted her hands in his hair and tugged him back with a sexy growl that made his knees weak. Then using the hungry slid of her lips and lusty strokes of her tongue, she proceeded to completely obliterate any kiss that had come before.

Any woman who had come before.

There was only one woman.

This woman.

Noelle.

A jingle penetrated his thoughts, followed quickly by—"Yoo-hoo! Anyone home?"

They jumped apart, then stared at each other in disbelief. Had he just kissed Noelle? Had she just kissed him back? He was still trying to come to terms with the answers when two Lab puppies came charging into the kitchen like wiggling balls of energy.

"Junie! Johnny! Get back here, you little rascals." Melba hurried in and tried to grab the puppies, but it looked like they had gotten good at escaping capture. Johnny Cash grabbed the muffin Noelle had dropped and ducked under a low shelf while June Carter headed for the pantry.

"Oh, no, you don't!" Noelle chased after the dog and scooped her up. Junie rewarded her with sloppy kisses. She giggled and cuddled the golden Lab close before she pointed at the thumping black tail sticking out from under the shelf. "Grab him, Case. Sheryl Ann will have a fit if she finds out dogs were loose in her kitchen."

Once he was down on the floor, he took a few minutes to breathe deeply and collect himself before he reached under the shelf and pulled the puppy out. As soon as he lifted the ornery guy into his arms, he got the same sloppy licks Noelle had.

"I'm sorry," Melba said. "The little scallywags jumped right out of the basket before I knew what was happening."

"It's okay." Noelle laughed as Junie gave her more kisses. "But we probably better get them out of the kitchen before a health inspector shows up." She headed into the front and Melba and Casey followed. Once there, she sat down on the floor and started playing with the puppy. Seeing his sister free and having fun had Johnny wiggling to get down. Casey set him on the floor and he raced over to join Junie and Noelle. There was something about watching Noelle playing with two puppies by the Christmas tree that made Casey's stomach feel all light and airy.

"So I saw your truck parked outside and figured you might be here," Melba said. "Have you talked with your daddy about taking Junie and Johnny?"

He pulled his gaze from Noelle and the puppies. "I'm sorry, Mel, but I've been a little distracted lately. I'll ask him tonight."

"Distracted?" Melba glanced between him and Noelle and he wished he'd used another word. "There's been a rumor going around town about you two. Of course, I've never put much store in rumors. I prefer to get my news from the horse's—or both horses' mouths."

Before Casey could reply, Noelle did. "I wouldn't put much store in the rumors, Mel." She pulled her apron tie from Junie's mouth. "Everyone in town should know better than to think Casey and I would ever get together."

It was the truth. So why did her words rub him wrong? Maybe because, only minutes before, they'd been kissing like they couldn't get enough of each other. But that had been a mistake. A huge mistake. He had come here today to get Noelle out of his thoughts, not to add more thoughts of her.

"That's what I told folks," Melba said. "But I guess people were just hoping for a holiday romance."

"Nope." Noelle firmly shook her head. "No romance here." Her gaze connected with his and her eyes sparkled with mischief. "And I'll be happy to take the puppies, Melba."

Casey should have thanked his lucky stars and left. He didn't need two more dogs. But he seemed to be on a roll of doing things he shouldn't do. "I'll take them. After all, I called first dibs."

"But won't your daddy skin you alive if you bring home two dogs without asking permission, Casey?" Melba asked.

Noelle smirked, which made Casey more than a little embarrassed and snappish. "I don't have to ask permission. I'll take the dogs."

Melba's eyes lit up. "Great! I have their food

and dishes back at the sheriff's office. If you swing by on your way home, I'll give you everything you need. In fact, why don't I just take these two rascals with me now so we can say our goodbyes." She scooped up the dogs and put them in the basket, hooking them to the leashes wound around the handle.

Which made Casey realize that Melba had planned the entire escape.

He was starting to wonder if Noelle was her coconspirator. Especially when a satisfied smile settled over her face once Melba was gone.

"So you're working with Melba now?" he said. "Conning people into foster animals?"

She laughed. "They're adorable, Casey—tricked into getting them or not. I'm sure Cloe will be thrilled when you bring them home."

"She'll be the only one. Sam will throw a fit and Rome is feeling a little stressed out about becoming a daddy so I doubt he'll be happy about dealing with two pup—" He cut off when she flipped over the closed sign. "What are you doing?"

Noelle glanced over her shoulder. "I'm closing up and don't want anyone interrupting me when I make my social media post about you no longer being my cowboy hero."

"You're doing that now?"

"I thought that's what you wanted."

It was. It was exactly what he wanted. Even if there was a niggling feeling in his stomach that said differently. "Great! I'll let you get to it." He grabbed his jacket off the rack and then glanced around for his hat.

"It's in the kitchen. I think I knocked it off when . . ." She let the sentence drift off.

"Right." He turned and headed into the kitchen. Sure enough, his hat was on the floor right next to the counter. He scooped it up, then headed back to the door where Noelle was waiting. He was almost through it when she stopped him

"Casey?"

He glanced over his shoulder to see a soft smile.

"Thanks for tasting my muffins."

Chapter Nine

ONE OF THE perks of driving home with two mischievous puppies was that Casey didn't have time to think about the kiss. He was too busy trying to keep Junie and Johnny from making him drive his truck off the road.

If they weren't scrambling onto his lap to give him sloppy kisses and sharp nips from their tiny teeth, they were ducking under the seats and then squealing because they couldn't get back out. He had to pull over twice to rescue them. The second time, he found a piece of rope in the boot and attached it to their collars, tying them to the passenger seat where they finally settled down. Junie went to sleep while Johnny teethed on the rope.

It was dark by the time Casey got home. He saw the light display long before he reached the house. The two-story ranch house could be seen from space. Multicolored Christmas lights hung from every possible branch, bush, eave, and rooftop. There were even lights on the barn and wrapped around the hitching post. Rome had outdone himself and Casey knew exactly who his brother had done it all for.

Cloe was no doubt thrilled and Casey couldn't deny that he liked it too. It was nice being the Griswolds for a change, instead of the Grinches.

He pulled up next to the brand-new white Cadillac SUV parked in front and wondered who was visiting. Since they didn't get many visitors, besides Cloe's family, he figured one of the Holidays had gotten an early Christmas gift. Whoever it was, Casey planned to thank them. His daddy wouldn't raise so much of a ruckus about the puppies with guests there.

He parked next to the SUV before glancing over at the puppies that were now sitting up in the seat and staring at their new Vegas lit-up home. "Now listen up, you two, the plan is to be as cute as possible with Cloe and Rome and as huntin' dog as possible with my daddy. Got it?"

But the puppies never got a chance to follow his orders. As soon as he walked in the door with them tucked under each arm, he realized his mistake. It wasn't one of Cloe's sisters and her husband sitting on the leather couch in the living room sipping on Sam's best brandy.

It was Melissa and her daddy the judge.

Johnny chose that moment to pee . . . all over Casey. He couldn't even blame the dog. It was a pissy situation. Casey had completely forgotten Melissa and her father were coming for dinner tonight.

He ignored the pee soaking into his jeans and

tried to brave his way through. "Pardon me. I forgot we were having guests tonight."

Sam, who stood by the fireplace, looked as hot as the fire. The judge and Melissa didn't look much happier. Or maybe that was just Melissa's resting bitch face. The constant sour look was one of the reasons Casey hadn't prolonged their relationship. That, and Melissa had been too calculating for his tastes.

"Oh, my goodness, would you look at those sweethearts?" Cloe came to the rescue and filled the awkward silence. She struggled to get up from the couch. At almost two weeks past her due date, she struggled to do a lot of things. Rome got up and helped her to her feet and they both came over to greet the puppies. Cloe gave him an are-you-trying-to-tick-off-your-father look and Rome smirked like he was thoroughly enjoying himself.

"Whose dogs are these?" Cloe asked as she scratched Johnny's ears.

Casey dropped the bomb. "Mine."

"Yours?" At Sam's gruff response, Junie decided it was her turn to release her bladder. Casey really should have taken the dogs to pee before he brought them in the house. Lesson learned.

Cloe realized his predicament and glanced at her husband. "Rome, why don't you take these sweet babies outside to the barn so Casey can go get cleaned up before supper."

Rome quickly did his wife's bidding. As he took the puppies, he lifted his eyebrows at Casey. "Melba?"

Casey wasted no time getting showered and changed. He knew he was in big trouble, especially when he glanced at his cellphone after getting out of the shower and saw all the text messages from Cloe, Rome, and his daddy asking where he was. But it wasn't the first time he'd been in trouble with his daddy and he figured it wouldn't be the last. It wasn't like he hadn't tried to get out of the dinner. His father should have listened when he'd said he didn't need him playing matchmaker. Now Casey would have to make it clear to Melissa that he wasn't interested.

The opportunity came much quicker than he thought. He had just pulled on a pair of boxer briefs when the door to his room opened and Melissa stepped in.

"Oops!" Her gaze swept over him from head to toe. "I guess this isn't the bathroom, is it?"

He knew Melissa well enough to know that she hadn't mistaken this door for the bathroom. This was confirmed when she walked in and closed—and locked—the door behind her. He pulled open the drawer where he kept his jeans, but before he could grab a pair, she stepped between him and the dresser.

She had changed her hair. In college, it had been a platinum blond. Now it was brown with a reddish tint. He had to admit it looked good. She was a beautiful woman . . . at least on the outside.

"My, how you've grown, Casey Remington." Her icy blue eyes ran over his bare chest. "So much more muscular and manly than I remember." She lifted a hand and ran one long French-manicured nail over his pec. The shiver that ran up his spine wasn't sexual, but she thought it was. A sly smile slipped over her lips, lips that were painted a muted pink that didn't tempt him nearly as much as a pair of candy apple-red lips.

Melissa finished outlining his man boob with her nail before she glanced up at him. "So what have you been doing with yourself, Casey?"

"Oh, same old, same old."

A knowing look entered her eyes. "Ahh. So you're still seeing how many women's beds you can get into before you die." She laughed.

That was one good thing about Melissa. She had never been jealous. Or clingy. When he had told her he wasn't interested in hooking up again, she'd only shrugged, blown him a kiss, and walked away. Which, hopefully, would make this entire awkward situation much easier.

"Pretty much." He pointed at the open drawer behind her. "Mind if I get dressed?"

"What's your hurry?"

"I can't really go down to supper in my underwear, Miss."

"I don't know why not. My daddy and your daddy would have a fit and we both love to piss off our daddies. Those puppies were a nice touch, by the way." Her hand slid down to his stomach. He grabbed it before those nails could slip into his boxers and do some damage.

"So if you love to piss off your daddy, I'm surprised you came tonight."

She stepped back and leaned against his dresser.

"There are times to annoy my daddy and times to see the benefits of a good plan."

"There are no benefits to dating me." He moved her out of the way and grabbed a pair of jeans from the drawer. "Something you need to make clear to your daddy." He pulled on the jeans and zipped them. "I'm sure he wouldn't want a womanizing playboy as a son-in-law."

She shrugged. "Daddy isn't interested in those types of traits. He's interested in connections that will help him win a seat in the senate."

The light bulb went on. This was why Sam was pushing so hard for Casey to marry Melissa. A judge in the family was nice, but a senator was even better.

"Your daddy runs one of the biggest ranches in the state," Melissa continued. "The Remington name holds a lot of respect and clout."

"Rome's and Sam's names maybe, but not mine. I'm just the carefree younger son who can't even be on time for supper."

She laughed. "No argument there. You never cared much for money or power. And it doesn't matter. Daddy and I will do all the caring. You just have to show up to the occasional fundraisers and political events and look pretty." She reached out and pinched his cheek. "You've proven that social media loves that face of yours."

His eyes narrowed. "What?"

"Don't play dumb, Casey. I know you carried a 4.0 all through college. You're smart. You just have no drive. And that's okay. I have enough drive for both of us. I want my daddy to win.

Not because I care one way or another about his political career, but because one day I plan to take his place. And I'm not only looking at a senator seat. I'm looking at the presidency. When I saw that chubby little baker's viral video, I realized you had the type of face and . . ." she made air quotes, ". . . 'cowboy hero' charisma to pull in, not only thousands of social media followers, but also thousands of young voters." She smirked. "It looks like that little baker realizes it too. Which is why she's been using you."

He didn't care about Melissa seeing the video. He cared about the other part. The crazy part. "You're behind the idea of us getting married?"

She tipped her head and gave him a wide-eyed look that was more scary than innocent. "Who do you think sold my daddy on the idea? I knew it wouldn't take much for him to persuade your daddy. In college, you spent one very drunk night telling me all about your daddy's desire to continue the Remington name—in between rambling about some girl you loved to tease in grade school."

"In case you didn't notice, Rome is continuing the family name."

"Oh, I noticed. It looks like Rome has quite the idyllic country life running this ranch. Perfect sweet little wife. Family on the way." She hesitated. "While you seem to be the extra son who really doesn't have a purpose. Yes, you're the charming brother-in-law and soon-to-be-uncle. But what happens five years from now when

Rome and Cloe have more kids and you're just weird Uncle Casey who doesn't have a life?"

Again, she did the scary wide-eyed look. "Or you can marry me and have your own life. A life that I can promise will never be dull. If you're worried I'm going to chain you to my bed, don't be. I have no desire to be stuck having sex with one person for the rest of my life either. Once we have a couple kids, you never have to touch me again as long as you can pretend like we're one big happy family in public and on social media. Out of the public eye, we can do what we please. Of course, I won't live on a ranch out in the middle of nowhere. You'll need to move to Austin. But I'm sure you'll love the big city where there are plenty of gorgeous women to keep you entertained."

She leaned in and rested a hand on his chest. "So what do you say, Casey? Should we kiss to seal the deal?"

Casey had never given much thought to the future. He was the type of person who lived in the present moment and let the future take care of itself. But Melissa had painted an extremely vivid picture. Of both scenarios. He had no desire to live in a big city and be married to some calculating politician who believed in an open marriage. He might not want a long-term relationship, but he had never slept with numerous women at the same time. Nor did he believe in breaking sacred vows said in front of God, your family, and friends. Not to mention using innocent kids for your image on social media.

But he didn't want to be Crazy Bachelor Uncle Casey either.

Rome and Cloe had never made him feel like he was intruding on their lives, but who would want your single brother living with you for the rest of your life? Rome and Cloe were starting their own family. While Rome might be used to Casey hanging around, Cloe wasn't. If Casey should have learned anything from his mama and Rome's first wife, it was that living with three Remington men wasn't fun and would eventually lead to divorce.

He didn't want that for his brother and Cloe.

"Casey?" Melissa pulled him from his thoughts. "What's the hesitation? Don't tell me you actually fell in love with that fat baker."

Casey wasn't sure what happened. One second, he was staring in horror at the future, and the next, he was taking the lifeline Melissa threw him.

"Now watch your mouth, Melissa. That's the woman I love you're talking about. Ellie isn't fat. She's perfect." That wasn't a lie. Her body had fit perfectly in his arms. Too perfectly.

The look of disbelief and anger on Melissa's face was damn satisfying.

"You're kidding me? You have a chance to marry me and you're choosing a silly little baker?"

He held up his hands. "Now don't take it personally, Miss. You had a great plan. And if I hadn't already found the love of my life, I might have considered becoming the first gentleman of the United States." When hell froze over. "But true love comes before country."

Melissa held up her middle finger. "Fuck you, Casey!" She whirled and stormed out of the room.

When she was gone, Casey sat down on the bed and blew out his breath. Damn. He'd really stepped into it his time. He'd been worried about people thinking he was in love and now he'd gone and confirmed it. He didn't doubt for a second that Melissa would broadcast the news to everyone she knew—including everyone on her social media.

Oh, how he hated social media. It really screwed with a man's life.

"What the hell did you do?" Sam came charging into the room. "Judge Matthews and Melissa just left."

Casey wanted to tell his father the truth, but there were some parts of the truth Sam wouldn't understand. Like Casey lying through his teeth. Sam hated liars even more than he hated Casey's carousing.

"I simply informed Melissa that I'm not interested in marrying her."

"Why? She's smart, beautiful, and seems to find your bad behavior amusing. At least, she did until you were so rude to her."

"Let's talk about rude, shall we, Daddy? Rude is inviting Melissa and her father here in the first place to play matchmaker. Or maybe that's controlling and arrogant more than rude."

"I wasn't forcing you to do anything. I was merely giving you an opportunity to make something of your life—an opportunity you were too stupid to take. Now I want you to pick up that cellphone sitting right over there and call Melissa and apologize. If you can charm every other woman in town, I'm sure you can charm Melissa into forgiving you."

"Sorry, but I can't do that. I'm not marrying Melissa." He paused and lied through his teeth. Or not really lied. Just stretched the truth. "I'm already seeing someone."

Sam stared at him. "Who?"

Before Casey had to answer, Rome appeared in the doorway. He didn't look like the calm, collected brother Casey knew. He looked panicked. And it wasn't over the judge and Melissa leaving before dinner.

"Cloe's having the baby!"

Chapter Ten

Noelle had been doing her live post when texts started popping up on the screen saying her sister was in labor. She could have quickly told her followers about Casey and her not working out before she signed off, but something held her back—probably the growing number of followers at the top of her profile page. So she excitedly told them about becoming an auntie before she waved goodbye and cut the feed.

When she arrived at the county hospital, she found most of her family in the waiting room ... including Casey Remington. Since she knew he would ask about her media post and she didn't want to get in an argument with him in a hospital waiting room, she decided to steer clear of him.

She played dominoes with Daddy and her brothers-in-law and took turns with her family checking on Cloe.

Cloe seemed to be handling childbirth like she did everything else—with calm strength. She breathed through each contraction and then once it was over, she talked to Noelle as if they were at Sunday dinner. Rome was a little more stressed. Each time a contraction hit, he looked more pained than Cloe. Of course, Noelle understood how he felt. It was hard watching her sister be in pain. It was a relief when Mama showed up to take over.

Mimi had been right. The fall from the swing *had* broken Mama's arm, but she hadn't let a cast slow her down. She came into the room like a whirlwind, issuing orders.

"Noelle, when you go back to the waiting room, make sure Sweetie doesn't overdo. We don't need another baby coming just yet. And keep your daddy from stress eating any more candy from the vending machine. And don't let Mimi fall asleep in an awkward position and get a crick in her neck."

"Sweetie and Daddy I can handle. Mimi's another story." Noelle blew a kiss to Cloe before she stepped out the door to do her mama's bidding. She froze when she saw Casey leaning against the wall.

"How is Cloe doing?" he asked.

"She's doing fine. Rome is taking it harder than she is."

Casey nodded. "You should have seen him as we were leaving. He was in such a rush to get to the hospital, he jumped into his truck and took off before any of us had gotten in." He glanced down. "Looks like you were in a rush too."

She followed his gaze and realized she still

wore her Santa apron. "Oh!" She laughed as she reached behind her to untie the strings.

He placed a hand on her arm and stopped her.

Heat spread from his fingertips through her body like a fast spreading wildfire. Her gaze went immediately to his lips. Lips she remembered all too well. Their softness. Their hunger. Their ability to wipe out every thought in her head but one.

Don't stop.

He was studying her lips too. His dark lashes hid his eyes, but she could feel their heat. They remained like that for what felt like forever before he removed his hand from her arm and cleared his throat.

"I was just going to say don't take your apron off. I like your aprons. They're . . . cheerful."

Before she could get over his compliment, a nurse came striding down the hall. She looked like she had a destination. Until her gaze landed on Casey. Then she stopped in her tracks. Noelle couldn't blame her. He looked like sex in a Stetson with the collar of his blue-jean jacket flipped up against his strong jaw, making his eyes look like two tropical wading pools.

But it turned out it wasn't his looks that had made the nurse stop and her eyes widen.

"You're the *Holiday Kitchen* cowboy!" Her gaze snapped over to Noelle. "Noelle!" She beamed. "Oh, my gosh, I just love your posts. Whenever I get homesick, I watch them. They make me feel like I'm back in my mama's kitchen with my best friend who is telling me all about her latest boyfriend." She shot a glance at Casey. "It makes me hopeful that I'll find my own cowboy hero someday."

Noelle waited for Casey to correct her. Instead, he did something that had her jaw dropping. He tucked an arm around her waist and drew her into his hard chest. He smelled good. Real good. Like fresh night air and virile man. His voice rumbled beneath her ear as he spoke.

"It's possible. Just look at Ellie and me." He kissed the top of her head. "A match made in baking heaven."

The nurse's eyes glazed over. "That's just so sweet. Wait until I tell the other nurses who's here." She turned and took off down the hall.

Noelle pulled back and looked up at Casey. "Just what in the world was that all—?"

Before she could finish, he took her hand and pulled her down the hall toward the elevator. Once inside, she started to repeat the question, but two guys in scrubs slipped in before the doors closed. Not wanting to talk in front of complete strangers, she waited until she and Casey stepped out into the lobby.

"Would you mind telling me what's going on?"

"In a second." He glanced at the waiting room that was still packed with Holidays. "I'd just as soon your family didn't overhear." Continuing to hold her hand, he led her out through the sliding front doors and into the chilly Texas night. Once they were outside, he turned to her.

"Did you already post about us?"

She thought about lying, but then realized he

could easily confirm it. "Not yet." The cold wind had her shivering and rubbing her arms. "I was getting ready to when I got the text about Cloe. If you're so worried about me posting, why did you make that nurse think we're together?"

He took off his blue-jean jacket and hooked it over her shoulders, surrounding her in cozy heat and manly scent. "Because I've decided to go along with your scheme."

She blinked. "What?"

He stepped back and grinned. "I've decided to be your rescuing, rose-delivering cowboy hero."

Her eyes narrowed. "Have you been drinking?"

He laughed. "Not a drop."

"So you want to explain why you've suddenly had a change of heart?"

"Maybe I'm just a nice guy who doesn't want to embarrass you about lying on social media."

"And maybe I'm Martha Stewart. Sell that to someone else, Casey Remington. You have never done a nice thing for me in your life."

"Now that's not true. I've done nice things for you."

"Really? What? Name one nice thing you've done for me." She tugged his jacket tighter around her. "Besides giving me your coat."

"I saved you from cracking your head open."

"That was just a split-second reaction. I'm sure if you'd had time to think about it, you would have let me fall."

His eyes squinted. "You really believe that? I know I've teased you over the years, but I would never want to see you hurt."

"You don't think all your bullying hurt?"

He drew back as if she'd slapped him. "Bullying? I never bullied you, Ellie. Teased, maybe. But never bullied."

"Well, sometimes teasing can feel an awful lot like bullying."

He stared at her in disbelief for a long moment before he spoke. "I'm sorry, Ellie. I didn't realize how my teasing made you feel."

She was so surprised by his sincere apology—an apology she never thought she'd hear from his lips—it took her a moment to reply. Even then it was a stupid reply.

"Well . . . okay."

His eyebrows lifted. "Well, okay? Does that mean you accept my apology and forgive me? Or does that mean you accept my apology, but still plan on making me pay?"

"I never made you pay."

"I don't know what you'd call it, Ellie. You scarred me for life with a pencil. You bad-mouthed me to every girl in town who would listen. You were constantly tattling on me to the librarian for talking too loudly and to teachers for cheating if my gaze even glanced in your direction. You told Mr. Crawley to keep a close eye on me because you thought you saw me putting a pack of gum in my pocket without paying. You even tattled to the sheriff about me and my friends setting off firecrackers in the dumpster behind the town hall and my daddy gave me a butt blistering I'll never forget. You made me pay for my teasing. Don't ever doubt it."

She wanted to deny everything, but she couldn't. She'd had a vendetta against Casey for a long time. Most of it was justified. But some of it was just her being hateful.

"You're right. I guess we both got a little carried away. Maybe we thought since our daddies were feuding, we needed to feud as well."

He shrugged. "Maybe. Or maybe we got to where we kind of enjoy it."

"I do not enjoy it!"

He grinned. "Oh, come on, Ellie. You can't tell me you didn't enjoy our feuding just a little bit. There's a sparkle in your eyes whenever you're yelling at me that doesn't match your angry words."

"It's called a sparkle of annoyance. And now that we've established you and I have been feuding, why do you suddenly want to be my social media boyfriend?"

The smile left his face. "My daddy has decided it's time for me to get married. If I'm already in a relationship, I won't have to suffer through his matchmaking."

"So you want to lie to your daddy?"

He frowned. "I already did. I didn't mean to. It just sorta happened."

She sighed. "Believe me, I get it. I didn't plan on lying to my followers either, but the penalty for being honest outweighed the benefits of perpetuating a lie."

He pointed a finger at her. "Exactly. And not having to deal with my daddy's matchmaking choices outweighs being stuck in a fake relationship with you."

"Gee thanks."

He laughed. "You're welcome."

"What about the rest of our family? Are we going to lie to them too?"

"It's not like we're getting married like Rome and Cloe did. We're just acting like we're dating. People date all the time and nothing comes of it."

She stared at him. "Other people date all the time. You've never dated in your life."

"Now that's not true. I've dated."

"You've taken a woman out to dinner or a movie or a concert? Some place other than the Hellhole for drinks and dancing?"

"Yes. In college, I took girls to parties."

"Took or met?"

"Met, but I still texted them to see if they wanted to go."

She rolled her eyes. "That doesn't constitute a date, Casey. And when you talk about dating me, are you talking about us actually dating or just pretend dating?"

"Just pretend dating. I'm sure you can make up some amazing dates for us to go on for your followers." He grinned. "The roses were a nice touch, by the way. I think this week you should buy yourself some expensive chocolates. Or maybe sexy lingerie."

The twinkle in his eyes made her realize he was teasing. The hilarity of the situation finally struck her and she laughed. An out-and-out laugh that seemed to take Casey by surprise.

But only for a second, then he joined her.

It was weird. It had always been Casey laughing at her and her getting angry. It felt nice to laugh together. He must have thought so too because when they finally sobered, he was still smiling. Not the teasing smirky smile he usually wore when she was around. This smile was as sincere as his apology had been.

"So are we doing this?" he asked.

The image of her followers count popped into her head and she knew the smiling cowboy in front of her was responsible for the huge growing number. "Yes, but we need to have some rules."

"I agree. There needs to be an end date. I'm thinking two weeks is plenty for me to be in a relationship."

"Two weeks?" She shook her head. "No. That's right before Christmas. That would be too upsetting for my followers to think I got dumped right before the holidays."

"You get dumped? Why do I get to be the bad guy? Why don't you dump me?"

"Because I'm the sweet little baker. I can't dump you and still keep my followers. But we could do a mutual breakup after the holidays."

He sent her a pointed look. "We just weren't right for each other? Sort of like what happened with your last boyfriend?"

She was more than a little surprised. "How do you know what happened between me and Kenny?"

"I watched some of your posts. From the comments I read, no one thinks it was mutual. They think you got dumped. Only people who get dumped say it was mutual."

She wanted to argue, but she couldn't. He was right. Kenny had dumped her and her followers all knew it. She was the only one keeping up the pretense.

"So what happened?" Casey asked. "Did he not like your baked goods?"

"Something like that."

He studied her. "I'm sorry things didn't work out."

"All things happen for a reason." She sent him a teasing smile. "Maybe I was just waiting for my cowboy hero."

His lips tipped in a sexy smile. "Maybe you were."

Once her gaze had lowered to his mouth—a mouth she had tasted—she couldn't seem to look away. Or keep herself from reaching up and gently running her finger over the scar. His lips parted in a puff of air and heated her finger . . . and her entire body. A need filled her. A need to kiss that scar and make it all better.

"Ellie?"

Her gaze remained on his mouth, desire swelling up inside her like a perfectly whipped soufflé. "Yes?"

"Maybe we should have another rule." His voice was deep and sexy and made her tummy tingle even more. But the heat of desire switched to the heat of embarrassment when he continued. "No more kissing."

Thankfully, before she could feel too embarrassed, the front doors swished open and Jesse stepped out.

"There you two are. I've been looking all over for you." He grinned brightly. "She's here! Autumn Grace Remington is here!

Chapter Eleven

Casey was having a weird dream.

He was sitting in a kid's desk in his old fifth-grade classroom... naked as the day he was born. Standing at the front of the class wasn't sweet old Mrs. Simons. It was Noelle. She was wearing one of those puffy white chef's hats, a double-breasted chef's jacket, and red cowboy boots. She looked sexy as hell. And extremely angry. Her green eyes were narrowed and her cherry-red lips tipped in a frown as she slapped the palm of her hand with a wire whisk. With each twang of the whisk, she spoke one word.

"You. Have. Been. A. Very. Naughty. Boy. Casey. Remington."

Casey felt naughty. Extremely naughty. He was hiding a major hard-on under the top of the small desk.

"And it's time to pay for all your bullying." She moved down the aisle and stopped next to him. *"Stand up and bend over your desk."* When he didn't comply, she brought the whisk down on the desktop. *"Now!"*

He hesitantly got to his feet, trying to hide his erection with his hands.

Her eyes narrowed. *"What do you have there? Are you hiding something from me?"*

"No, ma'am."

"Remove your hands and let me see."

Casey slowly removed his hands. Those green eyes widened before they lifted to him. A seductive smile curved those red lips.

"So you like me after all."

Casey shook his head. *"No."*

She leaned closer and whispered in his ear. *"Liar, liar, pants on fire."* Suddenly, he was bent over the desk and she was beating his bare butt with the whisk. It was painful and exciting all at the same time. *"Say it! Say you like me!"*

"I like you!" he yelled above the loud twangs. *"I like you!"*

The twangs turned to loud knocks and Casey startled awake. It took a moment to figure out he wasn't in his old classroom with a stinging butt and a major hard on. He was sitting in his truck in front of Crawley's General Store . . . with a major hard on. The knocking continued and he turned to Mrs. Stokes standing at his window.

He was thankful the woman was too short to see into his truck. He rolled down the window and pinned on a smile.

"Hey, Ms. Stokes." He glanced at the Crawley General Store sign that had been decorated with green Christmas garland and red bows before looking back at her. "Corbin found out you had an illicit affair with Mr. Crawley and will tell everyone in town unless you quit smoking?"

She rolled her eyes. "Everyone in town already knows I had an illicit affair with Delbert."

Casey stared at her. "Wait. You had a—"

She cut him off. "I'm not interested in talking about old news. I'm interested in why a man in his twenties is sleeping in his truck at nine . . ." she glanced at the ancient watch on her wrist, ". . . twelve in the morning? I thought you were dead."

"No, ma'am. Just exhausted. Autumn Grace has been keeping us up nights."

Autumn Grace was the tiniest little thing Casey had ever seen in his life. If Cloe and Rome hadn't issued numerous reminders about supporting her wobbly head, Casey could have easily palmed her in one hand like a basketball. But while Autumn Grace's body was tiny, her voice was big. Ever since she'd come home from the hospital, she'd kept everyone—but Sam who slept like the dead—up at night.

She hadn't been the only one exercising their lungs.

Junie and Johnny howled as loudly as Autumn every time Casey tried to make them sleep in the barn. He'd finally given up and snuck the puppies into the house every night after his daddy went to bed. When Rome and Cloe finally got Autumn quiet, the puppies decided it was time to play.

After three consecutive days with no sleep and

Rome's added workload, Casey was a walking zombie.

"Ahh." Mrs. Stokes smiled. "One look at that child and I knew she was going to be a pistol. Just like her uncle. I remember you keeping your mama up nights."

Casey always grew uncomfortable when people brought up memories of his mama. Mostly because he didn't have any. "I guess that's just part of having a newborn."

Mrs. Stokes studied him. "Looks like you're getting a taste of what it will be like when you have your own children."

"That's not happening anytime soon. I'm not even dat—" He cut off when he realized what he'd been about to say.

He *was* dating. At least, he was fake dating on social media. According to Noelle's posts, he had taken her to Austin for dinner and a concert, gotten into a flour fight with her while making sugar cookies, and enjoyed a romantic midnight picnic in the Holiday hayloft. He had to hand it to Noelle's acting ability. As he'd watched her live posts and listened to her excitedly go on and on about their imaginary dates, there was a part of him that wished he'd actually done those things with her.

She had a way of making dating sound fun.

He pinned on a smile and tried to fix his blooper. "What I mean is Noelle and I aren't dating seriously. We're just . . ."

"Having a little holiday affair? Or what do the young folks call it? Hooking up?"

"Umm . . . well—"

She cut him off. "No need to explain. I figured that out all on my own after seeing you two rolling around on the floor at Nothin' But Muffins." She winked. "Sometimes all it takes is a little friction to start a fire. Now I need to get to the bank and make some heads roll. I left the Christmas decorations to my assistant manager and he thought it would be a good idea to do away with a tree in the front lobby entirely because of messy needles." She snorted. "Young people today just don't understand that all beautiful things come with a little mess." She pointed a finger at him. "Before you head back to the ranch, you need to get yourself some caffeine. Sleeping behind the wheel when your truck is sitting is one thing. Sleeping while it's moving is something else entirely."

"Yes, ma'am," he said.

But Casey didn't have any intentions of going into Nothin' But Muffins. Especially after the weird dream and the even weirder thing that had happened outside the hospital the night Autumn Grace was born. Casey had never wanted to kiss a woman so badly in his life as when Noelle had touched the scar on his lip. And she had wanted to kiss him too. He had felt it in her heated touch and heard it in the huskiness of her voice. It had taken every ounce of willpower he had to deny himself the pleasure.

Kissing Noelle again was a bad idea. They didn't need to blur the lines of their fake relationship.

He got out of his truck and headed into Crawley's to get the dog crates, newborn diapers, and earplugs he'd come into town for. He ended up picking out bigger crates that Junie and Johnny could grow into so Mr. Crawley helped carry them out. As they were loading them into the bed of the truck, a cold breeze swept over Casey . . . bringing with it a titillating scent that had his heart beating faster and his saliva glands working overtime.

He wasn't the only one who noticed.

"Smell that?" Mr. Crawley tipped his balding head back and took a big whiff. "That's the scent of Christmas heaven."

The emotions the scent evoked in Casey weren't heavenly. It was hunger. Carnal hunger. It punched him so hard in the gut that he almost doubled over.

"Have you tried the new holiday muffin?" Mr. Crawley continued, completely unaware of Casey's struggles. "It's much better than that Fa-La-La Fruitcake. The plums are tart and sweet and the cake is warm and moist and that sugar topping just melts on your tongue like the most delectable—"

Casey didn't hear what else Mr. Crawley said. His senses were too wrapped up in the scent filling his lungs. The pull was too strong to resist. With only a mumbled thank you, he turned and headed across the street like a sleepwalking zombie.

It wasn't until he stepped through the door of Nothin' But Muffins that his brain registered where he was. But it was too late. Noelle had already spotted him. All his life those green eyes had registered hate when they landed on him. Today, they twinkled as if she was actually happy to see him. Everything inside him went a little topsy-turvy and his stomach dipped like he'd just jumped off a rope swing at full arc. The feeling only increased when a smile spread over her face.

"Hey, Case." When he just stood there too stunned to speak, her smile faded. "Are you okay?"

No, he wasn't okay. He wasn't okay at all. And things got even worse when Noelle finished with the customer she was waiting on and came out from behind the counter and took his arm. Her touch was both jarring and soothing all at the same time.

What was that all about?

"Come sit down," she said as she led him to a table. "I'll get you some coffee and a Sugarplum Fairy muffin. It looks like you need a little caffeine and sugar."

A few moments later, he had a warm muffin and a cup of steaming coffee sitting in front of him. The aroma of baking muffins was even more powerful in the café. And yet, the only thing he could smell now was the enticing cookie scent of Noelle as she sat down across from him. All he could see was the concern in her shamrock-green eyes.

"Cloe told me about Autumn keeping y'all up. I guess Cloe and Rome probably look as exhausted as you do?" When he didn't say any thing, she lifted the muffin, peeled back the paper wrapper, and held it to his mouth. "Eat."

He took a bite. It was as warm and wonderful as he remembered. Before he knew it, she'd fed him every single crumb and then handed him the cup of coffee. It had cream and plenty of sugar—just the way he liked it. Three sips in, he started to feel more like himself.

He took a deep breath and released it. "Thank you. I guess I was more tired and hungry than I thought."

She smiled. "I guess so. You okay to drive or do you need me to drive you home?" She glanced around at the empty café. "It looks like I have a lull."

"No, I'm fine. Like you said, I just needed a little caffeine and sugar." There was an awkward silence. Which was confusing. He'd never experienced an awkward silence with a woman in his life. He cleared his throat. "So I saw that we've been thoroughly enjoying ourselves."

She laughed. Since when did her laugh get so sexy? "I didn't realize what a romantic you are, Casey Remington."

He pulled his gaze away from her shining, smiling eyes. "Yeah, well, I guess it just took the right woman to pull all the romance out of me. Where am I taking you this week?"

"I haven't decided yet. I'm thinking to look at Christmas lights. Although it's probably too soon for that."

"If you want to see a light display, you should come out to the ranch. My brother has outdone himself." As soon as the words were out of his mouth, he wanted them back. What the hell was he doing? He needed her showing up at the ranch like he needed to continue sitting there. He didn't know what kind of spell she'd cast over him, but he wanted no part of it.

But it was too late. The invitation had already been issued.

"I might have to do that," she said. "I want to see Autumn anyway. Since the new muffin came out, I've been so busy here that I haven't had a chance to visit until after I close up and finish my post. By that time, it's too late to come calling. Although Sheryl Ann gets back in two days so I'll have a lot more free time."

He couldn't help noticing how the sparkle went out of her eyes. "I guess you're going to miss working here."

She nodded. "I can't wait to have my own bakery. But until then, I'll have to work for someone else . . . unless I can get some sponsors on social media. I've been doing a lot of brand name-dropping and hashtagging lately."

"I saw your number of followers is still going up."

She sent him a sassy look. "All thanks to my cowboy hero." She leaned over the table. "You have a few crumbs." Her finger swept over his bottom lip.

Before, Casey had felt like he was sleepwalking. Now, he felt like he'd stuck his finger in an electrical socket. His body surged awake like he'd downed an entire gallon of coffee. Noelle must have felt the same surge because she jerked her hand back as if burned.

His gaze locked with her wide green eyes, eyes that reflected the same emotions coursing through him. Confusion . . . and whole lot of heat. Before he knew what he was doing, he was leaning over the table. His lips were a mere puff of exhaled air away from her plump cherry lips when the bell over the door jingled. They jumped apart and he turned to find another set of green eyes staring back at him.

Except these eyes were filled with anger.

"What the hell are you doing with my sister, Casey Remington?" Hallie Holiday growled.

Since Hallie looked like she was about to start swinging, Casey jumped up from his chair and held out his hands. "Calm down, Hal. I'm not doing anything."

"Really? So you weren't just about to kiss her. Because it sure looked that way to me."

"We were not getting ready to kiss!" Noelle positioned herself between Casey and her sister. Which was cute but useless since she barely reached his chin. "I don't know what's going on, but you can't just barge in here and start yelling, Hal."

Hallie stared at her sister. "What's going on is that I just found out you and Casey have been seeing each other. Something you failed to mention last time we talked. What happened to never keeping secrets from your sisters, Elle? I believe that was a rule you came up with."

"I planned to call a meeting and tell everyone,

but then Cloe had the baby and things got busy here. Besides, it's not serious. We're just dating. I don't need to tell y'all every time I date someone."

Hallie rolled her eyes. "Really? I have heard about every Tom, Dick, and Kenny you have dated until I could puke, Elle. And now suddenly, you've become secretive? That seems awfully fishy to me." She glared at Casey. "And I have a few things to say to you too, mister. I don't care if you are Rome's little brother. After being dumped by her boyfriend, my little sister is vulnerable. The last thing she needs is some cowboy gigolo playing on her weakness and luring her into his bed."

"He's not luring me into his bed," Noelle snapped. "And even if he was, that is none of your business, Hal."

"It is when you're getting involved with one of the biggest flirts in Wilder."

Casey couldn't blame Hallie for thinking the worst. After all, he did have a reputation of being a flirt. But after Rome married Cloe, he'd thought the Holiday sisters would know him a little bit better—if not personally, then through Cloe. Now he had to wonder if Cloe saw him as just a carefree flirt waiting to defile the next unsuspecting woman too. Somehow the thought got mixed up with what Melissa had said about him being a useless part of the Remington Ranch. He suddenly felt like the worst human being to walk the face of the earth. He didn't like the feeling. He didn't like it at all.

"Maybe we need to tell your sisters—" He didn't get to finish before Noelle cut him off.

"No! We don't need to tell my sisters anything."

"And yet you can tell everyone about yours and Casey's relationship on your social media," Hallie said.

Noelle lifted her chin. "Maybe because the people on my social media are actually interested in my life and y'all aren't."

"Oh, great!" Hallie threw up her hands. "Here comes the drama!"

Noelle's cheeks flamed and her eyes flared with anger . . . and hurt. "This is exactly why I didn't tell y'all. Because you'd laugh and tell me how stupid I am or how dramatic I am. I have never been anything but the silly little sister who keeps y'all entertained. You have never, ever, taken me seriously. You think I'm just this frivolous kid who should be happy with a smile and a pat on the head."

"That's not true."

"Really? So you're saying you didn't think me quitting college to become a pastry chef was frivolous? You don't think my dream to be a social media influencer is frivolous? You don't think me falling in love with every Tom, Dick, and Kenny is frivolous?"

Casey could tell by the look on Hallie's face that she thought all those things *were* frivolous. Hell, Casey had too. But as he witnessed the hurt in Noelle's eyes he realized she didn't. She loved to bake. She loved talking with her followers on social media. And she loved to be in love. He probably had no business butting into Holiday sister business, but he couldn't stop himself.

"I don't think doing what you love to do is frivolous."

Hallie snorted. "Says the man who loves drinking and carousing at the Hellhole. Talk about frivolous."

"Leave Casey out of this, Hal," Noelle said. "He's done nothing wrong."

Casey didn't know who was more surprised by Noelle's defending him—him or her sister.

"Now I'm really worried," Hallie said. "You've never defended Casey in your life. Now suddenly y'all are dating? I just don't get it."

"Well, maybe you don't need to get it. Yes, I should have told you and our sisters that I was seeing Casey because sisters shouldn't keep secrets from sisters. But sisters *should* support sisters regardless of whether they think it's stupid or silly or frivolous." Tears glistened in her eyes, reflecting the lights of the Christmas tree. "Now you need to leave. This is my workplace. If you want to talk more about this, then call a Secret Sisterhood meeting. I'm done here."

Hallie started to argue, but then snapped her mouth closed. "Fine." Regardless of the argument they'd just had, she walked over and gave Noelle a hug before heading for the door. As she passed Casey, she shot him a warning look that pretty much said *Don't Mess With My Sister*. Casey gave her a brief nod, but it didn't remove the scowl from her face.

When she was gone, Noelle turned and headed

back to the kitchen. He figured that was her way of saying she wanted to be alone. He turned to the door, but froze when a sniff came from the kitchen.

Hell.

He found her sitting on a stool at the island with her face in her hands, her shoulders shaking with each sob. He pulled out the stool next to hers and took a seat. He had never been good with women's tears. Usually when they started crying, he made a hasty retreat. But as much as he wanted to leave, he couldn't leave her like this. Especially when she had taken care of him only moments before.

"I—wish—you'd—go." The muffled words came through her fingers.

He grabbed a nearby dishtowel and slipped it between her elbows resting on the stainless-steel counter. "Now what kind of fake boyfriend would I be if I didn't try to console my girlfriend when she was upset?" He hesitated. "If it's any consolation, I know how it feels to be looked at as the frivolous younger sibling. Of course, in my case, I am pretty frivolous. You, on the other hand, are not."

She lowered her hands. She looked a mess with her smudged makeup, blotchy face, and bloodshot eyes. So why did the sight of her tear-streaked face make him feel like pulling her into his arms and never letting go?

"Don't you lie to me, Casey Remington. You've always thought I was silly."

"Maybe when you were little. I mean those

rainbow tutus and huge hair bows you liked to wear were pretty silly." And cute. Very cute. "But I wouldn't call you frivolous now. Now you're just willing to go after what you want . . . even if what you want isn't what people think you should want. That's called guts."

She blinked at him. "You think I have guts?"

He nodded. "A lot more than I do. I've never had the guts to take a chance. To change my career, to put myself out there to be judged by a bunch of strangers . . . to make a commitment to one person. But you've done all those things. And yeah, maybe it seems frivolous to your sisters. But I think it's pretty brave."

She studied him for a long moment before she picked up the dishtowel and blotted her eyes. When she lowered it, she was scowling. "I'm really mad at you, Casey Remington."

He laughed. "Is that something new? What did I do this time?"

The scowl disappeared and her eyes softened. "You've been hiding a really nice guy under a teasing jerk."

Chapter Twelve

Of course, Hallie blabbed to the rest of the family about Noelle dating Casey. Noelle wasn't mad. They would have found out eventually. Especially when the townsfolk were all abuzz with the gossip.

Everyone took the news differently.

Like Hallie, the rest of her sisters were worried about her dating a man with commitment issues. Daddy grumbled about the possibility of having another Remington in the family. Mimi was delighted. Not only because he was a "charming rascal" as she put it, but also because he was a "helluva rancher." And Mama had yet to say anything.

As for the townsfolk, some people thought it was a joke, something Noelle had hatched up to get back at Casey for all his teasing. And most of those people were single women who didn't want to believe Casey Remington was off the market. But the rest of the townsfolk seemed thrilled that two of their favorites had ended up together. She'd overheard them calling it a perfect enemies-to-lovers story.

Not that she and Casey would ever be lovers . . . but the thought had crossed her mind.

If anyone had ever told her she'd be having sexual thoughts about Casey Remington, she would have laughed them off the face of the earth. But that was exactly what was happening. Every time she turned around, her mind was taking a trip down Casey Kissing Lane.

Probably because no man had ever kissed her like Casey. No man had ever made her feel like she didn't have control over her own body. From the first moment their lips touched, he'd controlled her like a puppeteer, every deep pull of his mouth and brush of his tongue tugging sexual strings she hadn't even known existed.

She knew it had to do with experience. Casey had probably kissed hundreds of women in his lifetime and the more you did something, the better you got at it. Noelle's first few piecrusts had been tough and inedible. After baking hundreds, they now melted in your mouth.

Mouth melting was a good description of Casey's kisses. Mouth melting and mind altering and body enflaming. She didn't doubt for a second that he'd be just as good at sex. A true sex expert—a *sexpert*—who could teach an inexperienced woman everything she needed to know to never embarrass herself in the bedroom again.

It was a crazy thought.

She was not going to let Casey teach her anything.

And yet, he already had taught her one thing: a

man can be the bane of your existence for most of your life, but all it took was the press of hungry lips for those feelings to change. Everything that used to annoy the heck out of her now turned her on. From the way his blond hair fell over his forehead as soon as he took off his hat to the way his Wranglers fit his butt.

And his hands . . . Casey had the best hands. They were tanned and strong, feeding into muscled forearms that made her stomach feel like a jiggly poached egg. When he'd brushed his calloused thumb over her lips, all she could think about was him using those hands to caress—

"The gingerbread men!" Mama hurried into the kitchen, pulling Noelle out of her sex daydreams. While Mama rushed to the oven and opened it, Noelle grabbed a mitt and pulled out the cookie sheet of charred, smoking gingerbread men.

"I'm so sorry, Mama," she said.

Mama fanned smoke from her face. "Well, there's no use crying over a few burnt men." She glanced around at the counters that were covered with gingerbread cookies and the pieces of the gingerbread house Noelle planned to make. "It looks like we have plenty. A few less won't make a difference."

Now that Sheryl Ann was back, Noelle had been helping her mama get a head start on the Christmas baking. They always made plates or tins of baked goods that they took to holiday parties or delivered to folks on Christmas Eve. Since Mama had one arm in a cast, she needed all the help she could get to make sure those plates were filled with yummy holiday treats.

It looked like Noelle wasn't being very helpful.

"But I'm a pastry chef. I should've known better than to daydream while I'm baking." Noelle pulled out the trash can from beneath the sink and dumped the cookies before setting the hot tray on top of the stove. When she turned, her mama was watching her intently with eyes the same green as all the Holiday sisters.

"So I guess you really like Casey."

Like was never a word that had applied to Casey and she still wasn't sure it did. But what she did feel was a little too R-rated to explain to her mama.

"I know it's weird," she said. "Especially with how much we disliked each other, but he's kind of grown on me." A concerned look entered her mama's eyes and Noelle quickly added, "But you don't need to be worried. I know you think I'm as fickle about love as the rest of the family. And I admit that I have been a little confused about what constitutes love. But I don't love Casey. We're just hanging out over the holidays. That's all."

It was easy to read the relief on her mama's face. "For the record, I don't think you're fickle about love, Noelle Carol. I think you have a big heart that loves easily. There's nothing wrong with that." She hesitated. "But there's a big difference in loving someone and being in love with someone. Sometimes you don't know the difference until it's too late and someone gets hurt."

Noelle wished her mama had told her this a long time ago. Before she had hurt her fair share of men . . . and Kenny had hurt her.

"Which is why I'm gonna be a lot more careful, Mama," she said. "No more jumping headfirst into love for me."

Mama patted her cheek. "Nice to hear, baby girl. It makes me feel better about asking you to help out Cloe and Rome."

"Of course I'll help out. I was planning on heading over for a visit as soon as I finished with these cookies."

Mama sighed. "I'm afraid they need more than a short visit. As you know, sweet Autumn Grace has her days and nights mixed up and no one in the house is getting much sleep. Mimi and I have cooked casseroles for them and gone over and done what we can." She held up her cast in the sling. "Which isn't much with this thing. I can't even pick the little darlin' up. And Cloe and Rome need more than just casseroles and the occasional helping hand. They need full-time help."

Noelle stared at her mother. "Full-time? You want me to sleep over there?" An image of her and Casey tangled up in sheets popped into her head and she quickly pushed it back out as her mama spoke.

"Of course not. You don't need to sleep there. Just go over every day and help your sister out as much as you can. She was in tears when I talked to her last night because she hasn't had time to put up a tree or do holiday baking. She so wants to make her and Rome's first Christmas special."

Noelle could understand that. Holidays were important to her family. Darla had always gone all out for every holiday with decorations, food, and celebrating. It made sense Cloe would want the same for her new family.

"I would have asked your sisters," Mama continued. "But Belle and Liberty are busy planning all their holiday events and Hallie has the ranch and Sweetie is much too pregnant—poor thing's feet have swelled to the size of soccer balls. I just thought, since you were no longer feuding with Casey, you wouldn't mind—"

Noelle cut her off. "I don't mind, Mama." She smiled brightly. "I'm going to give those Remingtons the best Holiday Christmas they've ever seen!"

An hour later, she was driving down the long drive that led to the Remingtons' house. Casey hadn't been kidding when he said Rome had decorated the outside. Every tree and fence post she passed was covered with strings of lights. Noelle couldn't wait to see how it looked at night.

The Remington Ranch was much larger than the Holiday Ranch, but the two-story house wasn't as country charming as the one Noelle had grown up in. Nor was the rustic wood barn that sat to the left of the house. The Holidays' barn was painted a bright red and Noelle's tummy always got a warm, cozy feeling whenever she returned home and saw the top of the roof peeking over the trees like a cheerful wave.

If Noelle ever had a barn, it would be red and every Christmas she would make her husband hang a big ol' wreath with a huge red bow over the hayloft.

Speaking of wreaths, as she pulled up in front of the house, she noticed that the front door didn't have one. And that just wouldn't do. Especially for a Holiday. When she got home tonight, she would get out her mama's glue gun, some pretty ribbon from Mimi's sewing containers, some old ornaments from the attic, and make her sister the best wreath ever.

The thought had her smiling as she parked and grabbed the container of gingerbread cookies she'd brought the Remingtons. But her smile faded when she got out of her car and saw Sam coming out of the barn.

Noelle had never spoken more than a few words to the man, even after Cloe had married Rome. Like her daddy, Sam was the strong, silent type and she'd always been a little afraid of him. That fear intensified when he saw her and looked like he'd just bitten into a rotten pecan.

"I guess you're here to see Casey."

Noelle forced a smile. "Actually, I'm here to help out."

His frown deepened. "With what?"

"With anything that needs to be done."

"Thank you, but we don't need any—" He sniffed the air. "What is that smell?"

Noelle held up the container. "Gingerbread cookies. Fresh from the oven. It's my mama's family recipe. And I don't like to brag, but they're the best gingerbread cookies this side of the Pecos."

A wistful look passed over his face. "I know. I've tasted your mama's gingerbread."

She wasn't surprised, seeing as how her mama made Christmas plates for everyone in town. "Then I'm glad I brought some to share."

He hesitated for only a second before he nodded and turned for the porch. She followed behind him, noting his dusty clothes and exhausted gait. He wasn't as tall as his sons, but Casey had inherited his wavy hair that curled up on the back of his neck. He held the door open for her and she stepped inside, hoping to see Casey's, Cloe's, or Rome's welcoming smiles. But no one seemed to be around. So she waited for Sam to hang his hat on the rack by the door and followed him into the living room.

A living room that looked like it had been hit by a tornado.

Someone had started decorating the huge fresh tree by the fireplace and stopped right in the middle. Boxes of decorations and strings of lights were scattered all over the floor . . . along with lots of other clutter—a baby swing draped with dirty burp cloths, two piles of laundry, a breast pump, pacifiers, coffee mugs, half-empty bottles of water, plates with old food, and a stack of books on infant care.

It looked like Mama was right.

The Remingtons did need full-time help.

Noelle didn't wait for Sam to decline it again.

Without saying a word or asking for permission, she handed him the container of cookies and got to work collecting the dirty dishes and taking them to the kitchen. The kitchen was in the same shape as the living room. The baby bottles and nipples drying on a rack by the sink were about the only things clean.

Since Noelle had spent the last few years cleaning kitchens, it didn't take her any time at all to get the dishes put in the dishwasher, the counters wiped off, the beautiful oak harvest table polished to a high shine, and the floor mopped. While the floor dried, she headed to the living room to straighten up. But Sam had already done it. The tree wasn't decorated, but the boxes of decorations and lights had been neatly stacked next to it and the laundry was almost completely folded.

Noelle moved over to the couch to help, lifting a tiny little onesie from the remaining pile. "So where are Rome and Cloe? Did they take Autumn Grace into town?"

"I thought so, but then I found them upstairs sleeping. I guess Autumn kept them up again last night." He smiled the first smile she'd ever seen from him. "That one is going to keep them on their toes. She reminds me of Casey. He hated sleep. Although he didn't fuss like Autumn. He was the happiest baby I've ever seen. He just didn't want to miss anything." He shook his head. "He still doesn't."

She couldn't argue. "He does enjoy life."

His smile faded. "So what's going on between you two? Casey is acting like it's serious, but he's never been serious about anything in his life. Which makes me suspicious."

She swallowed hard. "Suspicious? What do you mean?"

"I find it curious he suddenly found a girlfriend the minute I started pressuring him to marry Melissa Matthews."

Casey had mentioned his father's matchmaking. He just hadn't mentioned there had been a particular woman. She didn't know why the news made her feel angry. It wasn't like her and Casey's relationship was real.

"Ellie?"

She turned to find Casey standing in the doorway of the kitchen. He'd removed his hat and his hair was sweaty and messy. In fact, all of him looked sweaty and messy. Which didn't detract from his good looks one iota. The butterflies that filled her stomach felt real. Too real.

"She came to help," Sam said.

Casey released his breath and looked up at the ceiling. "Thank God." He walked right over and gave her a hug that made the butterflies even worse. He smelled like sweat, but also like fresh winter air and horses and leather. It was the most erotic scent she'd ever smelled in her life. When he released her, she wanted to dive back into his arms and bury her nose into his strong, corded neck and just inhale forever.

"I'm gonna go take a shower," he said. "Don't go anywhere, okay?"

All she could do was nod, then watch as he

headed for the stairs and took them two at a time, his butt filling out the Wranglers to mouthwatering perfection. When he finally disappeared upstairs, she snapped out of her daze and glanced over to see Sam watching her with an intent gaze.

Rather than explain her ogling of his son, she quickly made her excuses. "I think I'll get dinner started."

Since the entire freezer was filled with the casseroles Mama and Mimi had brought over, it didn't take much work to make supper. The only things she contributed were a chopped green salad with a red wine vinaigrette and some biscuits. She was just putting the biscuits into the oven when Casey walked into the kitchen. It wasn't his slicked-back wet hair that made her knees feel like she'd run a marathon. Or his freshly shaved face. Nor was it the way the blue Henley shirt hugged his biceps and made his eyes pop.

It was the tiny little baby tucked against his chest.

"Look who's up?" He kissed the dark peach fuzz-covered head. "It's Autumn Polly Doodlebug."

Noelle tried to ignore the way the sweet image melted the bones in her legs and moved toward them. "Aww, look at her." She held out her hands. "Give her to her Auntie Elle."

He drew back, his big hand cradling Autumn's head. "Now don't get demanding. There are rules and regulations that must be followed first. Did you wash your hands?"

"Of course. I always wash my hands numerous

times while I'm cooking." She went to take the baby, but he turned away.

"Do you have any sharp zippers or buttons on your shirt?"

"Does it look like I have any zippers or buttons?"

His gaze lowered to her T-shirt. Or more like her breasts. A long moment passed before he spoke. "It doesn't appear so."

"Just hand her over, Case," she snapped.

His gaze lifted and she saw the twinkle in his eyes. "Fine. You may hold her. Just support her head."

"I know how to hold a baby." She did. She had held a lot of babies in her life—just none that she had to take from a sizzling-hot cowboy who smelled like soap and shampoo . . . and baby lotion. He placed the baby on her chest and his knuckles brushed against her breast.

She couldn't remember how many times she'd walked across carpet in her stocking feet and gotten shocked when she touched a doorknob. The feeling that zapped her was similar . . . and completely different. There was that instant shock, but it was followed by a warm, glowing feeling that settled deep and low in her stomach.

As she stood there with a warm bundle of baby pressed to her thumping heart and staring into Casey's Grecian-ocean eyes, she knew.

She knew she was going to do another frivolous thing.

Chapter Thirteen

CASEY HAD CONFLICTING feelings about Noelle coming to help. Part of him was thrilled to have a clean house, his laundry washed, and dinner ready when he got home after a hard day of ranching. The other part was struggling to deal with having a woman he lusted after so close at hand.

Just one whiff of Noelle's bakery scent made him lightheaded and breathless. One glance from her evergreen eyes had him stuttering like a fool. And if she touched him, he was toast.

Petrified toast.

He'd jacked off so much in the last three days that he worried he'd done permanent damage. The worst part about it was it hadn't helped. She'd cast some weird spell on him that made him constantly horny but unable to find satisfaction.

"Casey?"

He pulled from his thoughts and realized everyone at the dinner table was looking at him. Especially Noelle who had just spoken his name.

"I'm sorry," he said. "What did you say?"

"I asked if you wanted more pecan pie."

Why did the word "pie" coming from her pouty red lips sound so sexual? All he could think about was diving into her warm, sweet—

"No!" He spoke the word so loudly that everyone at the table startled. He lowered his voice. "I mean, no, thank you. No pie for me." *No pie. No muffin. No sweets from Noelle period.*

Cloe stood. "Well, if everyone is finished with dinner, I think we should go in and finish decorating the tree before . . ." She let the sentence drift off, but everyone knew what she wanted to say. *Before Hellion Autumn Grace wakes up.* Casey adored his niece, but there was no denying she was a pistol. A screaming pistol who could wake the dead with her crying fits.

Casey got up and started collecting the dinner plates. "I'll do the dishes and let y'all start decorating." The less time he hung around Noelle, the better. Unfortunately, Sam seemed to like throwing him and Noelle together. No doubt because he wanted Casey to cave and confess that he'd lied about their relationship.

"No, I'll do the dishes." Sam got up from his chair. "You should spend time with your girlfriend."

Casey pinned on a smile. "Thanks, Sam. Nothin' I like better than being around Ellie."

The tree Cloe had ordered was at least twelve feet tall with full branches that took up the entire corner of the room. Which explained why it took Rome and Casey teetering on two stepladders with twelve strings of twinkle lights to cover it.

Once they'd plugged in the lights, Casey had to admit that the effort was worth it. Not only because the tree looked like an explosion of stars, but also because of the stars it put in the Holiday sisters' eyes. They stood in front of the tree with their arms hooked around each other and their faces lit with sheer joy.

Rome glanced over at Casey and grinned from ear to ear. Casey knew how he felt. He couldn't help the satisfied feeling that settled in his stomach. That feeling only grew as he watched the sisters gleefully start hanging the ornaments, exclaiming over every one. Including the box of ornaments Rome had taken down from the attic.

"Oh, my gosh!" Noelle held up the cotton ball snowman Casey had made in first grade. "I remember making these." Her gaze snapped to Casey. "I also remember a certain someone wiping his gluey hands in my hair." A comment like that was usually accompanied with a condemning scowl. So he was surprised when she flashed him a smile and a wink. "You were so ornery, Casey Remington." Thankfully, she turned back to the tree to hang the ornament before she could notice his reaction to that smile. His body flamed like the fire crackling in the fireplace.

"Look at this one." Cloe lifted a fragile-looking angel ornament from the tissue paper it had been wrapped in. She carefully wound the music box handle sticking out beneath one satin wing and the tinkling sound of "Angels We Have Heard on High" filled the room.

Casey didn't have memories of his mama

growing up, but this song had always struck a chord in him. Maybe because music embedded deeper in your psyche than visual memories. Or maybe because Rome had told him how much their mama had loved the song and sang it every Christmas. Whatever the reason, every time he heard it, it made him feel things he didn't want to feel.

He climbed down from the stepladder and set down the string of fake cranberries he'd been about to loop around the tree. "I think I better go check on Junie and Johnny."

Once outside, he took deep breaths of the chilly night air before he headed toward the barn. As always, Junie and Johnny were thrilled to see him. He sat down in the pile of straw in their stall and let them cover his face in sloppy kisses.

"Okay, okay, I love you too."

He grabbed a ball and threw it into the corner. They stopped showering him with attention and tumbled over each other to retrieve it. He continued to play ball with them until Junie's ears perked up and she bounded to the half-stall door and started barking. Johnny joined in on the barking. A second later, Noelle appeared.

She wore a coat and a red-and-green knit hat pulled low, only a few strands of dark hair peeking out. Her cheeks and nose were red from the cold, but he'd noticed at dinner that she hadn't painted her lips red today. They weren't painted at all. He didn't know what he liked better—the glistening cherry red or this soft natural rose.

"Well, hello, you two sweethearts." She opened

the stall door and stepped in. As soon as she sat down on the bale of hay, the puppies were all over her. She giggled with delight as they danced around her legs and jumped up to give her wet licks. After they had settled down, she looked at Casey. "I see they still have plenty of energy."

"Too much." Casey grabbed the ball and tossed it into the corner. Both puppies scrambled after it. Soon the two were wrestling around in the hay for possession of the ball. Both Casey and Noelle laughed. When they sobered, Noelle's gaze drifted to him.

"Rome told us about the angel being your mama's. You okay?"

"I'm fine. I just needed to check on these two."

She nodded and looked at the puppies playing. "Do you keep in touch with her?"

He really didn't want to have this conversation, but he couldn't see how to get out of it without Noelle thinking it bothered him. "We talk occasionally."

"That's good. I mean . . . she's your mama."

"Not really." The words just popped out. He wanted them back, but it was too late. When Noelle glanced at him in question, he shrugged. "She wasn't here for me, and the few times a year we talk, I get the feeling that it just makes her feel guilty. So I don't push a relationship."

"I'm sorry." The compassion in her voice brought a lump to his throat that was hard to talk around.

"It's not a big deal."

"Yes, it is. It's a very big deal to have a parent

who doesn't know how to show their love. My daddy has always struggled to show us girls how much we mean to him. Luckily, we have Mama and Mimi and each other to make up the difference. You just had Rome and your daddy. And I get the feeling that Sam is a lot like Hank."

"Gruff and unbendable?"

She laughed. "That's putting it mildly." Junie came back over for attention and she stroked the puppy's ears. "What I'm saying is that it's okay to be upset, Casey. It's okay to be sad that she left and angry that she still doesn't know how to be a mama. You don't have to smile all the time."

"I don't smile all the time."

She sent him a skeptical look. "Okay, then ninety-nine percent of the time. Your smug smile used to make me so mad I could spit. The more I tried to get back at you for all your teasing and pranks, the more you smiled. I thought you were like my sisters and only thought of me as a cute little nuisance whose sole value was to amuse you."

Her honesty took him by surprise and maybe that's what had him being just as honest. "I never thought of you as a nuisance. I liked making you mad, but only because I wanted your attention." He hadn't meant to be that honest. Her eyes widened with disbelief and he quickly tried to salvage his dignity. "I mean I was a greedy boy who loved having all the girls' attention." He grabbed the ball and tossed it again, hoping her attention would move to the two puppies tumbling head over tails as they scrambled to get it.

It didn't.

"Casey."

Just the breathy way she said his name made him burn. He tried to keep his eyes on the puppies, but it was impossible when she slipped off the bale of hay and moved toward him on her knees. With her on her knees and him sitting, they were eye level. So that left nowhere to look but into her meadow-green eyes. They had looked at him in a lot of different ways—mostly annoyance and anger. Now, they held a softness that drew him in like the warm glow of lit windows on a frigid night.

She lifted a hand and cradled his jaw in the warmth of her palm. "Well, you have my attention now, Casey Remington." She leaned in and brushed her lips over his.

The kiss was nothing like the kiss they had shared in the kitchen at Nothin' But Muffins. This kiss was feather soft ... and undemanding. Maybe that was what made it so powerful. Women had always had high expectations of Casey's sexual abilities. But Noelle's kiss held no expectations. Made no demands. It was just a gift freely given. After giving it, she drew back and smiled as if it had been everything she'd wanted.

"I think I like having your attention too, Case."

Those ruby-red nails slid through his hair, drawing him back to her rose-colored lips. This time, they parted and welcomed him into the heat of her mouth. He groaned low in his throat and came to his knees to get closer to the full-figured body that had been keeping him up at night. It welcomed him as much as her mouth, her arms hooking over his shoulders as she pressed all those sweet curves against him.

A flood of desire snapped his control and he took over the kiss, bending her back over the arm he had wrapped possessively around her waist as he hungrily fed on her mouth. He wanted to eat her whole and might have done so if two furry puppies hadn't wiggled their way between them, causing Noelle to giggle against his lips before he drew back. Her lips were puffy and wet from the kiss and her eyes twinkled.

"I'm really starting to think your dogs don't want us kissing."

Casey sighed as he tried to control Johnny and Junie who just wanted in on the new game. "I'm starting to think the same thing." He glanced at her. "And maybe that's a good thing."

The hurt look was easy to read in those green eyes. She stood and brushed the hay off her butt. "I guess I'm not as experienced at kissing as you're used to."

He quickly got to his feet. "It's not that at all, Ellie. It's just that I . . . well, I thought this was all fake." And what just happened hadn't felt fake. Not fake at all.

She hesitated before she completely blindsided him. "Maybe it doesn't have to be."

He stared at her, thinking he'd misunderstood. "What?"

"Maybe we could have a relationship . . . a physical relationship." When he was too stunned to speak, she elaborated. "Sex."

There was a long awkward moment before he released his breath in a huffy laugh. "You really had me going there, Ellie." When she didn't laugh, he sobered. "You're serious?"

Her cheeks flushed and she lowered her gaze. "I guess it is a foolish idea. I just thought you were feeling what I've been feeling. But obviously that's not the case." Her shoulders lifted in a weak shrug. "And why would you? Kenny proved that I'm not the type of woman men desire." She turned and headed out of the stall. "I better go help Cloe and Rome finish decorating the tree."

He stood there for only a second before he secured the puppies in the stall and chased after her. He caught up with her on the porch and took her arm, pulling her around to face him. The massive light display made the tears in her eyes look like a thousand colorful gems.

Gems that cut straight through his heart.

"You're wrong, Ellie. I don't know what Kenny's problem was, but it had nothing to do with you not being sexy. You're the sexiest woman I've met in my life."

She pulled away from him and shook her head. "You're just saying that to make me feel better."

"No, I'm not." He took her hand and placed it on the bulge in the front of his jeans. Just the feel of her hand had his semi turning full.

Her eyes widened and a puff of air came through her parted lips. "Oh."

Before he embarrassed himself, he removed her hand. "So sexual desire is not the reason I don't want to get involved in a physical relationship with you. I just think it would blur the lines of our fake relationship."

"But why? I mean if we both agreed that it would just be sex, then I don't see the problem. You have sex all the time and it doesn't mean anything."

He sighed. "But you don't."

Her eyes widened. "This is about me being a virgin? Because if it is, I'm not. Kenny took my blossom and then pretty much told me it wasn't worth the effort I'd taken to save it."

Casey was not a violent man, but he had the strong desire to hunt Kenny down and beat him senseless. "He sounds like an asshole who was trying to compensate for his own sexual insecurities."

"But don't you see? Whether it was Kenny's inexperience or mine, I don't want my next sexual experience to end up being another embarrassing failure. And if anyone can help me become experienced, it's you, Case."

Just the thought of helping Noelle become experienced had at least a thousand fantasies vying for a place in his head. Thankfully, his logic overruled them. She might say she wouldn't get attached, but he couldn't trust the word of a woman who had dressed up as a bride for Halloween all through grade school.

"I'm sorry, Ellie, but that is a resounding—"

A high-pitched wail came from the house and cut him off.

"Autumn Grace is up." Noelle turned to the door, but stopped before she reached it and glanced back at him. "Just think about it, Case. That's all I'm asking. Think about it."

As he watched her disappear into the house, Casey knew that's all he'd think about.

Chapter Fourteen

Operation Get Casey As a Sex Teacher was not going well.

Mostly because Casey was as good at avoiding her as he was at kissing.

For the last four days, ever since she had made her proposition, he had worked well past dinner. When he did finally walk in the door, he wolfed down the plate of food she'd saved him, thanked her graciously, and headed upstairs where he stayed until she left.

She might have thought he wasn't interested in her if she hadn't felt his interest. It had been a lot of interest. A lot of long, hard interest that made her weak just thinking about. Since he desired her and she definitely desired him, she didn't see why they couldn't have a holiday fling. A short holiday fling before she went back to Dallas, where she had been offered a job as assistant pastry chef for a prestigious downtown hotel.

The job offer had come just that morning. She should be thrilled. It was an amazing opportunity. Most new pastry chefs would be doing cartwheels about now. But for some reason, she wasn't. Probably because running Nothin' But Muffins had made her dream of owning her own bakery even more vivid.

That, and she would miss her family. She enjoyed waking up before sunrise and having coffee on the front porch with Daddy. Enjoyed helping Mama and Mimi bake and put up holiday decorations. Enjoyed cuddling Autumn Grace, even when she was fussy. And regardless of their continual suspicions about her relationship with Casey, she enjoyed hanging with her sisters.

"Sweet Lord, Elle." Liberty closed her eyes and chewed the bite she'd just taken of the Sugarplum Fairy muffins Noelle had brought to the Holiday Bed and Breakfast that morning. Liberty, Jesse, Belle, and Noelle were at the Holiday Sisters Events' office that was located above the carriage house behind the bed-and-breakfast. "These are the best things I've ever put in my mouth." Liberty glanced at Jesse, who sat on the couch next to her with their fat pug, Buck, snoozing on his lap. "Well, maybe not the best thing."

Jesse grinned and leaned over to give his wife a kiss. "Good to know, Libby Lou. Now quit talking naughty in front of your innocent little sister."

"If she's dating Casey, I doubt she's that innocent anymore." Liberty turned to Noelle, no doubt waiting for a confirmation or argument. Noelle gave her neither.

"Don't start, Lib. Just like it's none of my business what you do with Jesse. It's none of your business what I'm doing"—or not doing—"with Casey."

"Fine! But if you get hurt, don't come running to me."

Belle, who had been sitting at her desk and talking to a client on the telephone for the last fifteen minutes, hung up and turned to Liberty. "Of course she can come running to us, Lib. That's what sisters are for. They are not for judging or saying 'I told you so.'"

"Thank you, Belly," Noelle said. "Now why did y'all call me here? Don't tell me it was just to bring you breakfast."

"No, but breakfast is certainly appreciated." Liberty took another bite of muffin before holding it out for Jesse to take a bite. Buck roused long enough to open his mouth and catch the dropping crumbs. The smell of food finally roused Gilley, Belle and Corbin's huge dog, from his nap under Belle's desk.

Mickey Gilley and Buck Owens had both been Melba's rescue dogs. Gilley was some kind of doodle mix. He looked like a Muppet and was just as cute. He followed Belle everywhere unless someone had food.

He was sitting in front of Liberty in a flash of his furry tail.

Liberty held the muffin over her head. "Back, you beast. You're not getting my muffin." Gilley whined and gave her a pitiful look until she conceded. "Fine, but only a pinch."

"No, Libby," Belle said as she got to her feet.

"That's too much sugar. I'll get him and Buck a doggie treat." She pulled a bag from the coffee bar cupboard and gave each dog a few treats before she answered Noelle's question. "We invited you here to help us with a surprise." She glanced at Jesse. "A surprise for our husbands. So you'll have to leave, Jess."

Jesse rubbed his hands together. "I do love a surprise. Of course, this puts a lot of pressure on me and Corbin to reciprocate."

Liberty smiled slyly. "I bet our surprises are going to beat anything y'all come up with."

Jesse stood, then leaned down and gave Liberty a kiss. "Challenge accepted." He straightened. "Come on, Buck and Gilley. We have a Christmas surprise to plan." The pug followed immediately, but Gilley looked to Belle and wouldn't leave until she gave him the okay.

"Go on, Gilley. I'm not going anywhere without you."

When Jesse and the dogs were gone, Noelle looked at her twin sisters.

"Okay, what's this surprise and why am I being asked to help? I'm not going to Austin and buying you sexy lingerie. We aren't even close to the same size in the booby department." She proudly pushed out her chest.

Belle laughed as she took a seat next to Liberty. It never failed to amaze Noelle how much the twins looked alike. "Truth. But we don't want you to buy us lingerie. We want you to make us a cake for Christmas."

"Y'all know I'd love to, but how is that going to surprise your husbands? They've eaten my cakes before."

"It's not the cake that's the surprise," Liberty said. "It's what's going to be inside the cake."

"What do you want me to put inside it?"

Belle and Liberty exchanged glances before Belle spoke. "Something that announces to our husbands and the rest of the family that . . . Liberty and I are pregnant."

Noelle stared at her sisters. "What?" She glanced at Liberty. "But I thought . . ."

"I know." Liberty beamed. "I thought I couldn't get pregnant either, but I guess my endometriosis scars didn't keep my ovaries from doing their job after all."

Noelle hadn't known how bad Liberty's endometriosis had been until recently. Liberty wasn't a sharer. She was the type of person who kept her emotions in check and powered through whatever life dealt her. So Noelle had no idea how much she'd wanted kids until now. Her face held the same joy as Belle's, but tears streamed down her cheeks. And Liberty was not a crier. In fact, she hated tears. Seeing her so overwhelmed with emotion made Noelle start crying.

"Oh my gosh, y'all!" She quickly got up and joined her sisters on the couch. Soon they were all crying and hugging. "I know twins do everything together, but this is crazy."

Belle drew back and wiped at her cheeks. "Isn't it wonderful? Our due dates are only a week apart." She smiled at Liberty. "It's like it was just meant to be that our July babies will be almost as close in age as we are."

"July?" Noelle sighed. "That's just awesome, y'all. We have to incorporate sparklers or something Fourth of July-ish on, or in, the cake. You leave it to me. I'm going to make it the best pregnancy announcement cake anyone has ever seen. I'll sketch out a drawing for you and bring it by in the next couple days for your okay."

Liberty shook her head. "It will have to be next week. Belle and I have a wedding in Austin and Corbin and Jesse are coming with us."

"Our new house by Cooper Springs is almost finished," Belle said. "And Corbin and I are going to pick out furniture for it. We plan to move in right after the holidays." She rested a hand on her stomach. "Which is perfect timing. But you can still drop the drawing off while we're gone." She hesitated. "Libby and I were wondering if maybe you'd like to stay at the bed-and-breakfast while we're gone and keep an eye on Gilley and Buck. Mimi can watch Tay-Tay." Taylor Swift was Corbin and Belle's tiger-striped kitten, yet another gift from Melba. "But she can't handle Gilley and Buck too. And we can't ask Mama. She's already doing too much with her broken arm. It's okay if you can't. We can always kennel them."

Noelle was getting a little tired of helping her sisters out, but she couldn't stand the thought of Gilley and Buck being stuck in a small kennel while Liberty and Belle were gone. "I'll do it."

Belle jumped up and gave her a hug. "Thank you. I'll get you the keys."

Once Noelle had the keys in hand, she left her sisters and headed to Remington Ranch. She was just getting out of her car when the garage door opened and Rome's truck backed out. It stopped next to her and the passenger window rolled down.

"Hey, Elle," Cloe said. "Didn't you get my messages?"

She pulled her phone out of her purse and saw the line of text messages on the screen. "Shoot! I turned the ringer off last night and forgot to turn it back on. What's going on?"

"Autumn is sounding a little congested so we're taking her to the pediatrician. Sam and Casey are working in the south pasture and we won't be back until later this afternoon. So you don't need to stay. You've already done so much, Elle, and we can't thank you enough for all your help."

"You know I don't mind at all. Since I already have a roast thawing out in the refrigerator, I'll just put it in the Crock-Pot. That way you don't have to fuss with dinner when y'all get home."

Cloe glanced over at Rome. "Do I have the best sister in the world or what?"

"No argument here." Rome leaned over and smiled at Noelle. "Cloe is right. We can't thank you enough, Elle. I know Sam and Casey feel the same way." He hesitated. "Is everything okay with you and Casey? He's been spending a lot of time away from the ranch and we thought maybe . . ."

He glanced at Cloe and she finished the sentence for him.

"Y'all had gotten into an argument."

Noelle forced a smile. "No. Not at all. And you don't need to worry about me. Like I told you both, we're just hanging out together during the holidays. It's nothing serious. Now get my sweet niece to the doctor's and keep me posted."

Once they pulled away, she used the key under the doormat to let herself in. It was strange being in the house all alone. But also kind of nice. She plugged in the lights on the Christmas tree and then told Alexa to play some Christmas music while she prepared the roast.

She had learned a lot of fancy recipes for how to prepare beef in culinary school, but not one of them beat out simmering the meat on low in a Crock-Pot with rich gravy, carrots, and potatoes. After she started the roast, she did a little straightening and folded the pile of baby clothes she found in the dryer. When she came out of Autumn's room after putting the clothes away, she noticed the open door of the room across the hall.

Casey's room.

She couldn't resist taking a peek.

For some reason, she thought it would be a mess. Instead, it was much neater than her room at the Holiday Ranch. No clothes or shoes were strewn around and the king-sized bed was made perfectly, the navy comforter smooth as glass and the pillows stacked neatly against the oak headboard. The nightstand held a lamp, phone charger cord, and an ereader.

The ereader surprised her. She hadn't taken Casey for a reader. She glanced at the door before she picked it up and opened it with a swipe. The titles ranged from popular fiction novels to books on raising beef cattle and animal husbandry. She replaced the ereader on the nightstand and again glanced at the door before she opened the top drawer.

It held chargers, nasal spray, ChapStick, nail clippers, sore muscle cream, melatonin capsules . . . and a box of condoms. She pulled out the box and read the label.

Her eyes widened.

Ecstasy XL. Twenty percent larger than the standard condom. Lubricated and ribbed for her intense pleasure.

Just the thought of Casey giving her intense pleasure made her feel like a puddle of warm maple syrup. Of course, he hadn't bought the condoms for her.

"What are you doing?'

She jumped and whirled toward the door, dropping the box. Casey stood in the doorway with his cowboy hat pushed back and his eyes narrowed.

He crossed his arms and leaned in the doorway. "Well?"

"Umm . . . I was just . . . straightening up."

He glanced down at her boots that were surrounded by condoms. "My condoms?"

She felt her face heat. Instead of answering, she knelt and started putting the condoms back in the box. She couldn't help noticing how many there were. It was like he hadn't used any of them. Which made her extremely happy.

He walked over. "I'll get them."

"I made the mess. I'll clean it up."

He reached down and took her arm, effortlessly lifting her to her feet. "I said I'd get them." The feel of his work-worn hand on her arm made her a little lightheaded. Or maybe she was still lightheaded from reading the box of condoms. Whatever the reason, she swayed on her feet, causing his hand to tighten and concern to enter his eyes.

"Are you okay?"

Nope. She wasn't okay. She was sex doped by this hunk of virile cowboy and she wasn't going to be okay until she got him into bed. As luck would have it, there just happened to be a bed right behind her and a bunch of *for her intense pleasure* condoms scattered around her feet.

Unfortunately, he seemed to read her thoughts and quickly released her and stepped back.

"No, Ellie. Not happening."

"Why not?"

"Because it's a bad idea." He turned and strode out of the room, but she followed him.

"Why is it a bad idea? You're sexually interested in me and I'm sexually interested in you. Why can't we have a night of . . . sexual interest? Just one night is all I want. One night where you show me all the things I should already know."

He stopped and turned to her. "There's nothing you should already know, Ellie. Believe me when

I tell you that your inexperience isn't a turn-off. Kenny is a dick who needs his ass whipped. When you meet the right man, he'll be thrilled to teach you everything you need to know. But that right man isn't me. I'm not anyone's right man. You need to understand that."

"Then we're a perfect pair because I'm starting to think I'm not anyone's right woman. And maybe that's okay. Maybe neither one of us is ever going to find our other half. But that doesn't mean we can't have moments when we feel like part of a whole—moments when we don't feel so alone." She hesitated. "And when you touch me, Case, I feel like I'm not alone."

He stared at her for a long moment before he released his breath in a hiss. "Dammit, Ellie. Why do you always have to have the last word?" With a frustrated groan, he pulled her into his arms and kissed her.

It wasn't a gentle kiss. It was rough and needy and devouring. She loved it. She loved knowing he felt the same way she did—like a champagne bottle that had just been popped so all the bubbly sprayed out. Liquid heat rushed through her veins as he stepped her back and pushed her against the wall, the hard evidence of his desire digging into her stomach and causing heat to pool in her panties.

Coming up to her tiptoes, she rubbed against his XL length. It *did* give her intense pleasure, so did his hand slipping beneath her shirt and palming her breast. In other men's hands, she had always felt too big. In Casey's, she felt just right.

He must have thought so too because he groaned as he squeezed her abundant flesh in his strong fingers.

"Damn," he muttered against her lips. "I could come just like this."

She pulled his bottom lip through her teeth. "Good by me."

He drew back long enough to strip her shirt over her head. At second later, her bra cups were tugged down and her breasts swelled forth.

"Holy shit!"

She would have questioned whether his exclamation was good or bad if he hadn't dove right in and started worshipping them with kisses. Lush, tongue-brushing kisses that made her knees so weak she had to hold on to his shoulders or slip to the floor. When his tongue swiped over her nipple, she swore she saw stars.

"Casey!"

She felt his smile before he sucked her nipple into his hot mouth. The tight coil of need between her legs tightened almost painfully.

She bucked her hips. "Please, Case."

His mouth released her, his breathy words brushing over her nipple. "You want me to take care of that itch, Ellie?"

"Yes!"

She thought he would carry her to his room. Instead, he knelt in front of her and expertly unbuttoned and unzipped her jeans before tugging them down. Once he had one leg out of the pooled jeans, he hooked it over his shoulder.

"What are you—"

That was all she got out before his hot, wet mouth *did* make her see stars. Sparkly stars that went with the fiery ones that he ignited between her legs. She had thought he was an expert and he was proving it. Only an expert could bring her to the brink as quickly as he did. With just the right tongue flicks and suction, he sent her spiraling over the edge into a gasp-worthy, quivering orgasm that seemed to go on forever.

As it drew to a satisfying close, she opened her eyes and looked down to see him watching her with hot blue eyes that made her feel a wave of desire all over again.

With one last sensuous kiss, he slipped up her panties and got to his feet.

"Okay. So this is happening. But just like with our fake relationship, we need rules. Firstly, this isn't going to be a long drawn-out thing." He held up a finger. "One time and one time only."

She tried to focus on what he was saying, but it wasn't easy when her brain was orgasm fried. So she just repeated what he said. "One time and one time only."

"Secondly." His gaze lowered to her breasts and he swallowed hard. "Secondly . . ."

"Secondly?"

He shook his head as if to clear it and lifted his gaze. "Secondly, no cuddling or long talks or romance. This is just sex. Nothing more. Understood?"

She nodded. "Understood. Now will you take me to bed, Case?"

"No."

"No?"

"No. This isn't the right time. This was just . . . a preliminary trial." She liked preliminary trials. She liked them a lot. "If we're going to do this," he continued. "Then we need a place where we won't be interrupted." His gaze lowered once again to her breasts. "A place where I can devote every single second to your lessons."

A warm shiver of anticipation ran through her. She had just the place.

Chapter Fifteen

Having sex with Noelle was a horrible idea.

But if that was the case, then why did Casey wake up feeling so damn happy? He didn't get upset that Junie and Johnny woke him at the crack of dawn to go outside. He didn't mind at all freezing his butt off in the icy wind while he waited for them to do their business. In fact, when they were finished, he allowed them to race around the yard and terrorize the barn cats while he sat on the porch and laughed at their antics. Once he put them in their stall and got back inside, he took a long, hot shower and sang "Jingle Bells" at the top of his lungs until Rome knocked on the door and told him to keep it down because they had just gotten Autumn Grace back to sleep.

He switched to whistling and was still whistling when he headed downstairs. He cut off and froze on the stairs when the front door opened and Noelle blew in with the cold December wind.

She wore a puffy white down jacket and tight jeans. Her ebony hair was wind tousled and her cheeks pink . . . and her lips a ruby red that matched the sweater she revealed when she removed her coat and hung it on the coatrack by the door. His gaze took in the sweet curves of her butt before she turned and gasped with surprise.

"Oh!" She placed a hand on those luscious abundant breasts that he'd spent the night dreaming of. "I didn't see you there, Case."

He made his way down the rest of the stairs and stopped in front of her. The scent of cinnamon and warm baked bread straight from the oven surrounded him and he wanted nothing more than to press his face into those soft breasts and live forever. But he was the one who had made the rule of no cuddling. And with good reason. It was up to him to make sure the lines of what they planned to do didn't get blurred. They were meeting tonight at the Holiday Bed and Breakfast. He could do all his inhaling then. And only then.

One night.

Just one night.

He pinned on a smile. "Good mornin'."

Her face flushed an even darker pink as if she too was thinking of tonight. "Good mornin'." Her gaze lowered to his mouth for a split second—just long enough to send a shaft of heat through him—before she lifted her eyes and cleared her throat. "I thought I'd come early and bring y'all breakfast." She held up the plastic container he hadn't noticed until then. "I hope you like cinnamon rolls."

His gaze dropped to her ruby lips. "I like all sweets."

Those lips parted on a puff of air and her tongue swept out and turned the red to glistening cherry. A stupid logical rule suddenly held no value. What would it hurt to take one tiny taste?

He dipped his head, but before his lips met sweetness, the door of his father's study swung open. Even though they jumped away from each other, Sam looked like he knew exactly what they'd been doing—or about to do. Since they were supposed to be a couple, Casey hooked an arm around her waist and tugged her closer. It was strange how well she fit tucked under his arm.

"Mornin', Sam. Did you sleep well?" He grinned down at Noelle. "I sure did."

Sam glanced between them before focusing on Casey. "I'm glad, because while I finish the fences in the south pasture, you need to take some hands and move the herd out of the west pasture. Heavy rain is predicted for tonight and I don't want to lose any cattle if that ravine fills up. So there's no time for any . . . shenanigans."

He sighed dramatically. "Well, shoot. You know how I love shenanigans."

Sam scowled. "That's always been your problem." He grabbed his coat and hat from the rack and headed out the door. Once he was gone, Casey glanced down to see Noelle watching him intently, those green laser eyes looking right through him.

"He loves you, you know."

He dropped his hand from her waist. "Oh, I

don't doubt it. But he doesn't like me. Or respect me."

"Have you given him cause to?" Before he could feel too hurt by the question, she continued. "I get it. The youngest in the family always has to work harder for respect. But I get the feeling you don't work as hard at gaining your father's respect as you do at playing the irresponsible younger son."

"Maybe I'm not playing."

A soft smile tipped her lips. "I used to think that. I used to think you were all play and no work, but you work just as hard as Sam and Rome do . . . if not harder. Since Autumn Grace's birth, you've taken the lion's share of the ranch work. So yes, I do think you've taken the role of the carefree, irresponsible son just to tick him off. Just like you used to do with me." Her green-eyed gaze was intent. "But I'm not tricked anymore, Casey Remington." With that, she turned and sashayed into the kitchen.

The day that had started out so great, quickly turned to crap. Two of the ranch hands Casey was depending on to help him move the herd called in sick. One Casey believed, the other he was sure just didn't want to spend the day outside in the bad weather. When he hung up from the call, he turned to see Noelle standing in the doorway of the laundry room holding a basket of clothes.

"Problems?"

"Two of the ranch hands that were supposed to help me move the herd called in sick."

"I can help you."

He shook his head. "You don't need to be out in this weather. I'll get Rome to help me."

"You can't do that. Autumn Grace has a cold and kept him and Cloe up all night. They're sound asleep and we don't need to wake them. I helped my daddy in worse weather than this." She shifted the basket to one curvy hip. "Unless you think I can't do it."

"You haven't herded in a while, Ellie."

"Then it's about time I got back in the saddle and honed my ranching skills."

He had a choice. He could call his daddy for help or take Noelle's. He knew who he'd rather spend the day with.

By the time the other two ranch hands showed up, the temperature had dropped and dark clouds had moved in. They quickly saddled and loaded the horses into the trailer. When they were finished, Noelle came out of the house with thermal cups of coffee and plastic baggies of cinnamon rolls that she dispensed with a bright smile. She had borrowed leather gloves and a black Stetson. With the puffy white jacket, she looked like a cute little cowboy snowman handing out holiday cheer.

The cheer continued when she got in Casey's truck. She found a station that played Christmas carols and immediately started singing along, then cajoled Casey to join in. Damned if they didn't sound half bad on their duet of "Baby, It's Cold Outside."

When they arrived at the west pasture, the temperature was even colder. If it did rain, Casey knew it was going to quickly turn into ice. So he wasted no time getting things moving. He made sure to give the gentler horse to Noelle. Once everyone was mounted, he issued instructions.

"Luke, you take point. Danny, you take right flank. I'll take left flank. Ellie, you're drag."

"Thanks. I love eating cattle dust." She sent him a saucy smile before she impressively wheeled her horse around and took off toward the back of the herd.

Casey spent the rest of the morning worrying more about her than he did the cattle. But as it turned out, there was no need to worry.

He had never seen Noelle ranch. He'd only seen the fussy girlie girl who loved dresses and makeup and painting her nails. While he had always been captivated by that girlie girl, he was even more captivated by this skilled cowgirl who handled a horse as well as any of the ranch hands. She also knew how to handle cattle. She kept the slower animals moving with a swing of her rope and a cute little yip that made him smile every time she used it.

By the time they stopped for lunch, he was thoroughly impressed . . . and thoroughly turned on. There was something about her rope wielding and the way her sweet thighs gripped the saddle that had all kinds of fantasies popping into his head.

While he couldn't seem to keep his eyes off her, Noelle wasn't paying him any attention. She was too busy handing out the ham-and-cheese sandwiches she'd prepared for everyone, the same way she had passed out the coffee and cinnamon rolls—with a big smile and friendly chatter. Although she moved slower than she had that morning and he figured she was feeling the affects of being in a saddle for hours.

"You okay?" he asked when she came over to give him a sandwich.

"I'm fine."

This was proven to be a lie when a few minutes later she refused to join him and the other cowboys and sit down on a rock to eat.

Stubborn woman.

The rain didn't arrive until they had the herd moved and were heading back to the trucks and trailer. Like Casey had feared, it was more ice than rain and stung like hell. He rode as close as he could to Noelle to block it, but she was still soaked through by the time they got back. He had to yell at her to get into the truck when she started to help him and the ranch hands load the horses.

She had the heater blasting when he finally finished and climbed into the truck. An overwhelming feeling of contentment consumed him. He didn't know if it was the blessed heat that surrounded his shivering body, or the beautiful instrumental version of "Silent Night" coming from the speakers, or the soft smiling woman sitting in the passenger seat. All he knew was everything suddenly felt right. Like all the pieces of his life had come together in this perfect moment.

"You okay?"

Noelle's question pulled him out of his thoughts and he nodded. "Yeah. I'm good." He realized it was the truth.

On the way home, they sang carols again. He drove home as slowly as he could, wanting the day to never end. When they finally pulled up in front of the barn, Noelle turned to him.

"I used to hate driving cattle, but that was fun."

It had been. It had been the most fun he'd had in a long time.

If ever.

Since he'd sent the ranch hands home, Noelle insisted on helping unload and unsaddle the horses. She was in one stall taking care of a horse and he was in another drying off Domino, when Sam and Rome showed up.

Neither one looked happy.

"What were you thinking, Case?" Rome said. "I just found out Jeb and Dale called in sick. You should have woken me up to help instead of taking Cloe's baby sister out in this weather. Cloe's been worried sick."

"That was totally irresponsible, Casey," Sam snapped.

Since they were right, Casey didn't argue. He shouldn't have taken Noelle out in this kind of weather. But before he could agree with his brother and father and apologize, she strode into the stall like a green-eyed avenger.

"Casey didn't take me out in this weather. I volunteered—or more like forced myself on him. I'm not some baby sister who needs to be protected from a little rain. Nor does Casey need his big brother's approval to make a decision on his own." She turned her attention to Sam. "And I don't think a man who has given his life to this ranch is irresponsible. I think he's loyal and hardworking and a man any father and brother should be proud of . . . even if they're both too arrogantly stubborn to see it! Now if y'all will excuse me, I'm going home to change out of these wet clothes." She glanced at Casey. "Thanks for the fun day, Case." She whirled and stomped out of the stall.

Stunned silence ruled before Rome spoke.

"It would appear that all Holiday sisters know how to put a man in his place." He looked at Casey, his eyes contrite. "She's right. I'm sorry for doubting you, little brother. I was just worried about you both being out in this weather." He placed a hand on Casey's shoulder. "But you're a grown man. You can handle a little bad weather and any job on this ranch as well as I can. Sometimes I—" He glanced at Sam. "We . . . forget that. Don't we, Daddy?"

Sam hesitated for a moment as if he was going to say something. But all he did was grunt before he turned and walked out of the stall.

Rome looked at Casey. "I'm pretty sure that was a grunt of agreement. He really was worried when the storm hit. It's just hard for him to say it."

But Casey wasn't concerned about Sam being Sam. His entire thoughts were wrapped up in Noelle defending him with such a vengeance. There was a moment when Casey thought she was going to pop his daddy right in the nose. That made him feel like . . . maybe he wasn't the screwup of the family. Maybe he was worth something.

That feeling stuck with him as he finished with the horses and headed to the house where Cloe had dinner waiting. Cloe didn't mention a word about Casey taking Noelle out in the weather so he figured Noelle had given her sister hell too. After eating, he headed up stairs to take a long, hot shower. When he stepped out, his phone pinged with a text from Noelle.

I'm at the Holiday Bed and Breakfast. Door's open. Noelle Room.

A few hours ago, he was ready to spend one night of passion in her arms. But that was before he had spent the day with her. Before he'd herded cattle with her. Before he'd sung carols with her. Before she'd stood up for him.

Before she had become something more than just a one-night stand.

He didn't know what that something was, but he did know that he couldn't take advantage of her. And that's what spending the night with Noelle would be—him taking advantage of her innocence.

Now all he had to do was explain that to Noelle. Somehow he didn't think she was going to take it well.

All the way to the Holiday Bed and Breakfast, he went over what he was going to say. He had the words memorized by the time he pulled up in front of the two-story mansion that had once been Mrs. Fields Boardinghouse, one of the most notorious whorehouses in central Texas. Which was why it was so ironic that Noelle had chosen it as the place she wanted Casey to teach her all about sex.

It had been years since he'd been to the mansion. Back then, it had been a falling-down old house he and his friends had brought girls to in order to scare them. Scared girls had a tendency to cling to the boy closest to them. Now the mansion had been completely renovated by Jesse Cates. The foyer looked like something that belonged in a swanky hotel. A swanky hotel from the 1800s. Jesse had brought the huge chandelier hanging over the foyer, the marble floors, and *Gone With the Wind* curved staircase back to life.

Casey might have taken a moment to look in some of the other rooms on the main floor if a huge, mangy mutt hadn't come charging toward him, almost knocking him over in his enthusiasm.

"Hey, Gilley!" He was giving the huge beast ear scratches when he heard whines coming from the back of the house. He followed the sound to the kitchen where Buck stood behind a gate with his curly-tailed butt wiggling with excitement. As Casey leaned over to greet the fat pug, Gilley jumped the gate to be with his friend.

Casey laughed. "Obviously, this gate is no match for your long legs, Gilley man." After giving both dogs some more attention, he left them and headed upstairs to find Noelle.

Cloe had told him about the rooms being named after each of the Holiday sisters. As he walked down the hallway, he read the brass plates by each door. *The Sweetheart Room, The Clover Room, The Liberty Room, The Belle Room, The Halloween Room* . . . and *The Noelle Room.*

The door was open. He hesitated for only a moment before he stepped inside.

The room was decorated like a Christmas card. The walls were a deep ruby, the curtains were a velvet pine green, and the settee was upholstered in a holly print that mixed both colors. There was a framed print of a Santa cowboy driving a sleigh filled with presents and a cut tree through thick snow. Another of a big red barn, similar to the Holidays', decorated with lights and a huge wreath. There were snowman pillows and Santa knickknacks and a tiny little lit tree sat on a table in front of the window.

The light from the tree was the only light in the room.

Which was why it took Casey a moment to find Noelle.

His daddy had never read him fairytales or gotten him Disney movies. But Casey had watched *Snow White and the Seven Dwarfs* at a friend's house. He had thought Snow White had just been a cartoon character, but as he moved over to the bed, he realized he'd been wrong.

She *did* exist.

The real version was even more breathtakingly beautiful.

Noelle's black hair looked even blacker against the white pillowcase. Her complexion even creamier. Dark lashes rested just above cheeks that were tinted a soft pink. But the feature that held his attention the most were her lips. Lips painted the same color as the walls and the holly berries and the Santas. Lips that drew him like no other lips had ever drawn.

His resolve to resist her melted like the icy rain that had fallen earlier.

If he only had one night with a princess, he wasn't about to refuse it.

Even it didn't make him a prince.

Chapter Sixteen

NOELLE WOKE TO the most wonderful sensation. She opened her eyes and fell into the blue of a Grecian sea. She felt like she was drowning, but in a good way. The sea was taking her breath, but giving her life. Every single cell in her body was buoyant, tingling, and alive . . . all from the soft lips resting on hers.

"Ellie," those lips whispered before they parted and she was consumed by lush, wet heat.

No one kissed like Casey kissed. If he wasn't flambéing her with devouring lips and hungry licks, he was simmering her over low heat with slow, mind-altering sips.

Like now.

There was no rush. He kissed her like they had all the time in the world—like it was the only thing he wanted to do . . . forever. Every pull of his lips and sweet stroke of his tongue was leisurely and intoxicating. Like sipping a fine wine and then suddenly realizing you were drunk.

Noelle was drunk on Casey's kisses.

She couldn't put one thought together besides *Please don't stop.*

To ensure that he didn't, she slid her hands into the thick waves of his hair. His hair felt like corn silk slipping through her fingers. If her body hadn't started making demands, she might have been able to stay right there, playing with his hair and kissing him for the rest of her life. But the simmer he'd started was quickly turning into a rolling boil. If she just had this one night, she wanted to experience everything.

She drew away from his lips. When they chased hers, she fisted his hair and tugged him back. "I want to see you naked."

His eyes widened for a fraction of a second before heat darkened them. "I think that can be arranged."

He leaned in and gave her a deep, lush kiss before he rolled to his feet. His gaze held hers as he slowly unbuttoned his flannel shirt. Beneath, he wore an off-white Henley that hugged his shoulders and muscled chest. But it only gave a peek at what lay beneath. When he stripped the shirt over his head, Noelle felt like she'd been slapped right in the lady parts.

Casey had one of those runners' bodies that made women veer off the road. His muscles were long and lean and . . . everywhere. There wasn't a tiny little speck of fat on him. Which wasn't good because Noelle had more than just a speck. Her sudden fear about Casey seeing her body had her mouth working without her brain.

"It's just not fair."

"Excuse me?"

She sat up. "It's not fair that a man who eats

sweets like you do can have a body like . . ." She waved a hand at his chest. "That!"

If he had laughed, she would have gotten up and socked him. But he didn't laugh. He didn't even smile. Instead, he said something that made her heart feel like it was floating.

"I'm sure everyone thinks the same thing about you. Which is why I'm really looking forward to seeing all those luscious curves stripped bare so I can give them the attention they deserve. So you want me to continue? Or should we start working on that cute little cherry dress you have on?" His gaze raked over her in a heated slide that made her tingle from head to toe. "I love that dress."

She tried to calm all the tiny tingles his gaze made her feel and leaned back on the pillows. "Continue . . . please."

This time, he did smile before his hand went to the button of his jeans. She had been so busy looking at all the naked muscles in his upper body that she hadn't paid much attention to his lower. There was an impressive bulge lifting the zipper of his fly. When that zipper slowly inched down, black boxer briefs—the same briefs Noelle had washed and folded—were revealed. Of course, they looked much different on Casey than they did in a laundry basket. They sat low on his tight stomach, hugged his hips and muscled thighs, and gaped open in the front to reveal a tempting peek of something hard and smooth.

"You want to unwrap me, Ellie?"

The words were spoken in a low, husky voice

that made her insides feel like heated honey. She realized she did want to unwrap him. She wanted it in a bad way.

She sat up on the edge of the bed as he moved closer. She hesitated. Would this end like her night with Kenny? Would she mess it up somehow and embarrass herself?

"Just do what you feel like doing, Ellie," Casey said. "There are no rules."

His words released some of her fears. This wasn't Kenny. She looked at Casey's impressive erection. Nope, nothing like Kenny. She, tentatively, reached out and slid a finger down the hard ridge beneath the soft cotton. It must have been the right thing to do because he groaned. Feeling braver, she outlined the shape of him before she took him in hand and gripped him through his briefs. The sound that came out of his mouth was more of a growl than a groan, but it spurred her on enough to hook her fingers in the elastic waistband and tug it down.

What sprang out was definitely XL.

It was extra long and extra virile and extra . . . extra. She felt lightheaded just looking at it. Not only from lust, but also fear. How was this going to fit? Especially when Kenny had been half this size and had struggled to get it in. Her fear must have shown because Casey slipped a hand along her jaw and lifted her face until her gaze met his. She saw desire, but she also saw understanding and some other emotion that instantly calmed her.

"Ellie. We're only going to do what you want

to do. You want to touch me. Touch me. If you want me to only do what I did yesterday. That's all we'll do." He hesitated. "But if you want more, I'll give you more. I'll make it good, Elle. I promise I'll make it good."

She believed him, but there was more to it than that. "Don't you see? I want to make it good for you too and I don't know how to do that."

He glanced down at his erection and back at her. "I think you're doing just fine. And this isn't a test. You're not being graded. The first time two people are together, it's always a learning experience. We're learning together, Ellie." He smiled. "Just like we did from kindergarten through high school. If I remember correctly, you were always a faster learner than I was."

"Because I paid attention while you were busy messing around—usually coming up with something to tease me."

His eyes sparkled with deviltry. "Because it was so much fun." His eyes darkened. "You want me to prove it?" He lowered to his knees, his thick erection brushing her calf. His gaze locked with hers as he placed his hands on her bare thighs just below the hem of her cherry dress. He squeezed ever so slightly, his calloused fingers like brands that took her breath away. "You want me to show you how much fun teasing can be, Ellie?"

His hot fingers inched up, pushing her dress as they went and leaving behind a trail of fire. "You want me to tease you until you scream?" When her dress was all the way to the top of her thighs, he stopped and sucked in a breath. "Oh, Ellie, you naughty little girl. Talk about a tease." His gaze lifted to hers and the heat she saw in his eyes made her feel weak and strong all at the same time. "You don't have on any panties."

She had spent a good hour deliberating on whether or not to wear them. Now, looking into his darkened eyes and feeling the hard length of him twitching against the inside of her leg, she knew she'd made the right decision. His hands slid to her knees and he gently spread her legs, exposing her to his hungry gaze.

His chest rose and fell as he heavily inhaled and then exhaled. "Oh, Ellie, please let me tease you."

She never thought she would say her next words. "Tease me, Case. Please tease me."

He did. He teased her with an expertise that completely rocked her world. Starting with soft butterfly kisses on the inside of her knee, he moved toward the juncture of her legs, the kisses becoming longer and including wet flicks of his tongue.

Between each kiss, he spoke. "Your skin—tastes so—fuckin' sweet. It's like—licking sugar—off a muffin. Of course—I can't wait—to eat the muffin."

Noelle couldn't wait either. She was soaked and throbbing and needed release in a bad way. But Casey hadn't been kidding when he said he was going to tease her until she screamed. When he hit the spot where thigh met pelvis, he completely bypassed the place she needed him the most and kissed his way down her other leg.

"Casey!" She slipped her fingers through his hair and tugged him where she wanted him.

He chuckled. "Such a greedy girl. What am I going to do with you?" He sighed, his warm breath falling against her wet center in a puff of heated air that had her hips bucking. "I guess I'll just have to give you what you want." He hooked his hands beneath her knees and lifted her legs, pushing her back on the bed until her thighs touched her chest. Talk about exposed. But she didn't feel more than a moment's embarrassment when his mouth settled on her, his tongue brushing close, but never exactly where she wanted it.

She tugged on his hair and wiggled her hips, trying to get him to the spot, but he evaded her attempts and kept right on circling until she quivered with need and throbbed with an ache that made her scream out in frustration.

"Casey!"

A second later, his mouth hit the spot, his tongue flicking in just the right way to send her flying.

It was like being struck by lightning and becoming part of the charged current. She felt bright and electric and powerful. Tightening her fists in his hair and her thighs around his head, she rode out the perfect storm.

He brought her back with light brushes of his tongue. When she had her wits enough about her to glance down, she found him watching her, his blue eyes intense and holding the same emotion she'd seen earlier. But this time it didn't fill her with calm. It filled her with a need to touch him like he had touched her.

"I want you inside me."

He drew back, releasing her legs. "You sure?"

She sat up and smoothed his hair that she'd messed. "I'm sure." She unzipped the side zipper before pulling her dress over her head. Once it was off, she wondered if maybe she should have worn a bra. Her breasts were a lot to take in all at once and Casey did seem a little stunned. After a few awkward seconds, she started to cross her arms, but Casey stopped her by cradling both breasts in his hands.

"Oh, no. I'm not done admiring these sweet . . ." He gently kissed one nipple. "Perfect . . ." He kissed the other nipple. "Glorious beauties." Moving from one to the other, he lavished them with open-mouthed kisses and hot sweeps of his tongue that had Noelle's insides melting and her head lolling back. His fingers found their way between her legs and before she knew it, he had her close to another orgasm.

But she didn't want to fall alone.

"No," she croaked out.

He drew back immediately, his eyes confused. "Did I hurt you?"

She shook her head. "No. I just want you with me this time."

He smiled. "I'd like that too." He got to his feet and finished removing his boxers. She scooted back on the bed as he took the wallet from his jeans' pocket and removed a condom. This part had been just another awkward moment with

Kenny. But with Casey, it wasn't awkward. It was sexy.

The way he tore the package open with his teeth. The way he wrapped his hand around his shaft and held it steady as he expertly rolled it on. When he lifted his gaze and caught her watching, he tipped his head.

"You okay?"

She nodded. "I like the way you do that."

His eyes darkened and he moved toward her like the blatantly masculine male he was. She expected him to climb on and get straight to business—it wasn't like he hadn't spent plenty of time getting her ready. But instead, he slipped next to her, lying on his side and bracing his head in his hand as his gaze slid over her.

"If I had known what you were hiding under those cute little aprons, Noelle Holiday, I would have worked much harder at getting them off." His fingers traced over her breast, circling her nipple and making it tight and achy.

"No, you wouldn't have. You didn't like me, remember?"

"You didn't like me first."

"That's not true. I liked you from the first time I saw you strutting down the street after your daddy and brother. I said *hi*, and if I remember correctly, you stuck your tongue out at me."

He stopped tracing her nipple and looked stunned. "I did not."

"You did too. I was crushed."

He studied her for a long moment before he spoke. "Girls used to scare me. I guess it had to do with living in an all-male house. And you scared me the most because I thought you were as pretty as the picture I had of my mama." He hesitated. "I wasn't enough for her so I guess I thought I wouldn't be enough for you."

The raw truth he'd just handed her made her heart feel like a cracked sphere of blown sugar. For the first time, she looked into his ocean-blue eyes and saw all the hurt and pain. Hurt and pain she wanted to heal. She rolled to her side and cradled his face in her hand.

"You're enough, Casey. You're more than enough."

She kissed him.

She kissed the determined little boy who had been trying so hard to keep up with his daddy and big brother—was still trying so hard. She kissed the insecure teenager who had chased after every girl—searching for the love his mama couldn't give him. And she kissed the hopeful man who just wanted to be enough.

When kissing couldn't express all the emotions his words had brought to the surface, she made love to him.

Chapter Seventeen

Casey knew the moment everything changed. The moment when the kiss was no longer just a kiss—when it turned into something more. Something that didn't just feed the sexual desire that had been prodding him for the last few weeks. This kiss fed a deeper need. One he didn't even know existed until Noelle's sweet lips and gentle caresses filled it.

He knew in his soul she would be the only one who ever could.

While that thought scared him, he wasn't willing to waste a second of being with her now on thoughts of losing her later. Especially when she pushed him back to the pillows and kissed her way down his body.

She wasn't experienced or skilled, and yet, every brush of her lips and stroke of her fingers made him tremble like he had never been touched by a woman before. And maybe it was more that he'd never been touched by *this* woman before.

She'd been so hesitant at first. She wasn't hesitant now. When she reached his nipple, she circled it with her tongue in a sweep of fire before tugging it into the hot, wet flames of her mouth.

He groaned and dug his head back in the pillow as he tried to hang on to his sanity. But sanity completely slipped away when her hand moved lower and gripped his condom-sheathed cock. She held him firmly, but, at the same time, hesitantly. As if she didn't know what to do next.

His body knew. His hips jerked, pumping into her fist. She quickly caught on and rubbed him from base to tip. His groan was guttural and he worried he wouldn't make it through another stroke. He placed a hand on hers and stopped her.

"Wait."

She released his nipple and looked up at him with confusion clouding her green eyes. "Did I do something wrong? It doesn't feel good?"

"Just the opposite. It feels too good." When the truth dawned, a smug smile spread over her face. He couldn't help laughing. "Feeling cocky, are you?"

Her fingers tightened and he groaned as she gave him a full stroke. "I think that's the pot calling the kettle black."

He allowed her to bring him to the edge with a few more tight pumps before he stopped her again. "I want to be in you when I come, Ellie."

The smoldering look in her eyes scorched right through him. She gave him one more squeeze before she released him and leaned up to kiss him. "I want that too."

Her words were music to his ears, but with them also came a helluva lot of responsibility. He rolled her over, but hesitated when he was positioned to enter her sweet heat. "I want to make this good for you, Ellie. So if anything hurts or just doesn't feel right, you need—"

She pressed a finger to his lips. "You've already made this feel good, Case. So just shut up and finish what you started."

He tried to take it slow, but it wasn't easy when the first feel of her tight heat had him wanting to thrust so hard he broke the bed. The only thing that held him back was the thought of hurting her. He took his time easing in and pulling out in shallow thrusts, watching her face for any signs of discomfort. When she crinkled her button nose, he froze.

"Is this hurting you?"

"No. I just thought . . ." She shook her head. "It's nothing."

"No, it's something. We're not continuing until you tell me what's going on."

She bit her bottom lip. "It's just that I thought sex would be a little more . . . intense with you."

Talk about his ego being slapped down. It was lying out on the floor, crying like a baby. "You want intense, Ellie. I'll give you intense. But if it hurts, you need to tell me. Okay? No keeping secrets."

"O—" That's all she got out before he thrust deep. Oh shit, it felt good. So damn good that he had to take a few seconds to collect himself or things would be over too quickly.

"You good?" The words rasped out of his throat.

She nodded. "It doesn't hurt. I just feel . . . full."

Her words had him squeezing his eyes shut. That's how he felt. Encased in her body, he felt full. Abundant. Overflowing. Complete. He eased out just a little and then shifted his hips and thrust until he was seated deeply. A satisfied *ahh* fell from his lips at the exact same time as one fell from hers. Her green eyes held a look similar to how he felt.

Awed.

Who would have thought that Casey Remington and Noelle Holiday would fit so well together.

And not just well.

Perfect.

He enjoyed the feeling for only a moment before his body started clamoring for release. He pumped into her, slowly at first, and then faster as his need for friction grew. It was hard to stay focused when sheathed in tight heat that set his body to trembling with every sweet clinch. But he refused to reach climax without her—refused to not give her what she deserved.

It was obvious she was enjoying it. Her head was pressed back, her lips parting with every erratic breath. But it was also obvious by the way she squirmed beneath him that he wasn't meeting her needs.

"Tell me what feels good, baby," he panted. "Tell me what you need."

She bucked her hips. "I need . . . I don't know!" He stopped pumping and pulled out of her. She shook her head and grabbed his arms. "No!"

"I'm coming right back, baby. I'm just going to

make it feel better." He grabbed the pillow next to her head. "Lift your hips." When she complied, he tucked the pillow under her hips, tilting them at just the right angle. When he thrust into her this time, the choked moan she released told him everything he needed to know.

She no longer squirmed. Instead, she wrapped her legs around him and met every thrust with one of her own. Her back was arched and her pupils dilated with passion and orders came out of her mouth like a drill sergeant.

"Oh, yes, like that! Just like that! Faster! Harder!"

The beauty of her claiming her sexuality was the thing that sent Casey over the edge. Try as he might he couldn't hold back. His entire body trembled with the force of the orgasm that hit him. As he closed his eyes and pumped out his pleasure, Noelle tightened around him and screamed out her release. Which only added to the waves of hot desire that flooded through him.

By the time it was over, he felt completely drained . . . and completely content. That contentment only grew when he melted down into the soft body beneath him. He only intended to stay that way for a moment. He was much too heavy for her. But then Noelle wrapped her arms around him and held on like she never wanted to let him go.

He didn't want to go anywhere either. He would have been satisfied to stay with his face pressed into her sweet-smelling neck forever. But only seconds later, her soft words fell against his ear.

"That. Was. Awesome."

His heart cracked open and confetti shot out as he pushed up to his forearms. "You liked it?"

"Liked it? I loved it! It was amazing, Casey. No wonder women are falling all over themselves to get you into bed."

The confetti dropped like bullets. He didn't like Noelle bringing up other women so casually. He didn't like it at all. What had happened tonight wasn't ordinary. He hated that she thought it was.

"It was never like this, Ellie," he said. "Never."

For one heartbreaking second, he thought she wasn't going to believe him. But then her eyes filled with a sparkling happiness that brought back the heart confetti.

"I'm glad." She slipped her fingers through his hair and drew him down for a deep kiss. It was shocking how quickly she had him hardening again. When she pulled back, the sultry look she gave him made him even harder. "But I think we can top it. Wanna try?"

There was nothing he wanted more.

Casey hadn't planned to stay long at the Holiday Bed and Breakfast. He'd planned to stay only long enough to scratch the itch that had Noelle's name written all over it. But as the night went on, he discovered the more he scratched the itch, the more it itched. It was close to eleven and three mind-blowing orgasms later when he realized the itch wasn't going away. The realization should have scared him, but it was hard to be scared when he had Noelle's soft body tucked against him.

She made him feel invincible and powerful. Like there wasn't anything he couldn't achieve.

Even being loved by a woman.

"What are you thinking about?" she asked as she drew lazy circles in the middle of his chest.

Not ready to divulge his thoughts, he quickly searched for another answer. The pretty wrapped presents under the little Christmas tree gave him one. "Your birthday is coming up. I was wondering what you wanted?"

She lifted her head and looked at him with surprise. "You know when my birthday is?"

"December twenty-fourth. So answer the question. What's your birthday wish? Wait, I bet I know what it is. You want to own your own bakery."

"True." She settled back against him, continuing to draw lazy circles with one cherry-tipped finger. "But that's more of a dream. Dreams you are responsible for making happen. Wishes are more of something you hope happens."

His fingers stroked up and down her arm. How did she get skin so damn soft? "So what do you hope happens?"

She hesitated before she spoke. "I want a real birthday party."

"You've never had a birthday party?"

"Not with friends. My birthday lands too close to Christmas so I always just celebrated it with my family. No one wants to come to a birthday party on Christmas Eve."

"I would have come if you'd invited me."

She stopped circling and propped her chin on

her hand, her green eyes twinkling up at him. "You would not have. Even if you had wanted to, your daddy wouldn't have let you. Our daddies were feuding, remember?" She hesitated. "Do you know why?"

"No. Both Rome and I asked, but Sam never gave us a real reason."

"Same with my daddy." Her gaze locked with his. "Maybe like us, they just didn't take the time to look deeper." A soft smile tipped her lips. "I'm glad I looked deeper, Case."

His heart took an exhilarating ride down a slip and slide. "I am too."

She placed a kiss on his chest, over the spot that now ached, before she snuggled against him and sighed contently. A few moments later, he heard the even breathing of sleep.

He had told her no cuddling, but there was nothing on God's green earth that could have made him move from that spot.

He woke to Noelle's squealing. He sprang out of bed with fists clenched, ready to battle whatever villain had snuck in during the night.

But there was no villain.

Noelle was sitting on the opposite side of the bed talking on her cellphone—although her gaze was on him. Her eyes twinkled with humor and he figured he must look pretty silly standing there buck naked with his entire body posed for a fight. He released his fists and crawled back into bed, sliding over to the warm woman who was just as naked as he was. Her breath hitched as he straddled her hips and nibbled his way along her bare shoulder.

"No, I'm fine, Mama." She tried to swat him away, but he wasn't going anywhere. "Yes, I'll see you soon." After she hung up, she melted into his arms for a brief second before she pulled free and stood. She took his breath away and he couldn't help reaching for her again. But she stepped out of his reach.

"Sorry, but I have to go. Sweetie's gone into labor." He started to get up, but she shook her head. "There's no need for you to leave. You can stay as long as you want." She headed to the closet and disappeared inside, then reappeared a moment later in sweats and fuzzy boots. "Just lock up when you leave." She walked to the door, but then stopped and turned back around. He was hoping she'd say something about the amazing night they'd just shared and ask when she could see him again. She did neither. "And do you mind letting out the dogs before you go and checking their food and water? Thanks! I owe you."

Then she was gone.

He sat there staring at the empty doorway and feeling like . . . the last heel of bread in the bag. He knew he was being silly. Her sister was having a baby. She had to go be with her sister. And he was the one who had set the guidelines of one night and one night only. So he shouldn't feel upset she hadn't asked him to go with her . . . or even kissed him goodbye. He should be happy she had made it so easy for him to walk away.

But he didn't feel happy.

He felt miserable.

He knew there was no way he was going to fall back to sleep. So he got up and got dressed, then went downstairs to let out the dogs and make sure they had plenty of food and water. The miserable feeling grew even worse on the way back to the ranch when his brain decided to replay every moment of his and Noelle's time together. Every kiss. Every caress. Every gasping orgasm. She had come to him for instruction, and yet he felt like he'd been the one who got schooled—the virgin who was taught what a real night of passion felt like. After Noelle, he now knew that all the other nights with all the other women had just been emotionless sex.

And that was the defining variable.

Emotions.

Somehow, tonight, he had let emotions get involved and he was paying the price.

Since it was around three in the morning, the house was dark when he got home. He pulled into the garage and quietly came in through the mudroom, trying not to wake anyone—especially Autumn Grace. As he headed for the stairs, he noticed the flickering light coming from beneath the door to his father's study. His daddy got up early, but not this early.

Concerned, Casey tapped softly on the door before opening it and peeking in.

Sam was asleep on the couch in front of a low-burning fire. Since Casey had been warned often enough about wayward sparks causing fires, he moved into the room to bank the coals and make sure the screen was properly closed. After he finished, he turned and noticed the framed photograph lying on the floor next to the couch. He walked over and picked it up. Since his father had never been the sentimental picture-cherishing type, he didn't know what to expect. But it certainly wasn't a picture of Noelle and Rome.

Confused, he looked closer.

No, not Noelle and Rome. Darla Holiday and Sam. They had to be no more than eighteen or nineteen. Sam had his arm around Darla and was looking at her like she hung the moon while she was looking into the camera and smiling a smile almost identical to the soft smile Noelle had given Casey that very night.

"What the fuck?" He spoke loud enough to wake his father. As soon as Sam sat up, Casey turned the photograph to him. "What is this?"

"None of your business." Sam got up to take the picture from him, but Casey jerked it out of his reach.

"Tell me what this is, Daddy." Since he rarely called his father by the title, it seemed to get Sam's attention. He stopped trying to take the framed photograph from Casey and dropped his hands to his sides.

"It's what it looks like. It's a picture of me and Darla Ford."

"Darla Holiday, you mean? You dated her?"

"Briefly. In high school."

All the pieces of the puzzle came together. "That's why you and Hank hate each other."

"Among other things."

"But that's what started it. She chose him over you."

Sam shrugged. "It happens. Nothing I can't handle."

Casey held up the photo. "Which is why you sit around mooning over this." A thought struck him. "You were in love with her?" Sam's silence was answer enough. He stared at his father in disbelief. "That's why Mama left, isn't it? You were in love with another woman."

Sam sighed. "Your mother left because she realized she didn't want the life of a rancher's wife."

"But she would have stayed if you had loved her." His voice grew louder as his anger and hurt swelled. "She would have stayed!"

"She wouldn't have stayed, Casey. Nothing would have made her stay."

"You could have! If you had loved her, you could have!"

Rome came charging into the room in his underwear. "What the hell is going on? Autumn Grace is sleeping and I'd just as soon she didn't wake up until Cloe gets back from the hospital."

"What the hell is going on? That's a good question, brother." Casey threw the photograph as hard as he could at the fireplace. Before the glass shattered, he was heading for the door. "Why don't you ask Daddy and Darla Holiday?"

Chapter Eighteen

Whereas Autumn Grace had screamed her way into the world only hours after Cloe had arrived at the hospital, Holly Joy came in without a peep a good fourteen hours after Sweetie went into labor. She had a halo of see-through golden fuzz and eyes that stared inquisitively at anyone who held her as if to say "And you are?"

"I'm your Auntie Elle." Noelle touched her tiny little wrinkled hand that rested on the receiving blanket swaddled around her. "I'm the one you'll come to for advice on pretty much everything—fashion, baking, social media, boys."

Hallie leaned over Noelle's shoulder. "Not boys, Holly. We don't want you serial dating like Auntie Elle."

Any other time, Noelle would have been offended by the comment. But even after a sleepless night, she was just too happy and content to care. Not only because she was holding her beautiful new niece, but also because of the time she'd just spent with a handsome cowboy who had taught her the difference between sex with the wrong guy and sex with the right one.

Kenny had made her feel cheap, humiliated, and ugly.

Casey had made her feel unique, worthy, and beautiful.

Even as inexperienced as she was, she knew the night they'd shared hadn't just been sex. It had been so much more. She was a little too gun shy to put a label on what he had made her feel. Probably because Hallie was right. She had been a serial dater. And even worse, a serial faller in love.

But this felt different.

What Casey made her feel was completely different than what all those other men had made her feel. She had cared about those men and enjoyed being with them. But not one of them had evoked the intense emotions that Casey did.

And always had.

Ever since she'd known him, her feelings for him had been strong. She'd spent her life telling herself that it was hate, but now she realized she'd just been lying to herself. She hadn't hated Casey at all. She'd hated the way he held her attention whenever he stepped into a room. Whether it was their kindergarten classroom or the Hellhole bar, he became her entire focus. At any age, she could have described his entire wardrobe in detail, from his favorite Wilder Wildcats football jersey with the frayed neckline to his favorite pair of jeans with the hole in the back left pocket. She'd known when he got a haircut and when he needed one. She'd known when he first got acne. Started shaving. Grew an inch. Developed muscles.

If his name came up in nearby conversations, she'd stop whatever she was doing to eavesdrop. Usually, it was girls talking about their dates with him. Jealousy had been her constant companion. She'd labeled that jealousy hate and made him out to be a bully. The truth was that she'd been the bully. She had treated him like her worst enemy, bad-mouthing him every chance she got, tattling to teachers if he so much as spit on the sidewalk, calling him an emotionless womanizer and much worse.

He never once got angry back. Never once lost his teasing smile.

Even when he was hurting.

Until recently, she hadn't realized how much he'd been hurting. But she should have known. She should have looked past the teasing smile and carefree lover boy and seen the lonely boy who hadn't had the motherly love she'd grown up with. She couldn't imagine what her childhood would have been like without her mama and grandma to soften the gruffness of her daddy.

Casey hadn't had that. He'd dealt with his motherless life the only way he knew how—by smiling and looking for the softness and love he craved in the arms of women. How could Noelle possibly blame him for that? How could anyone blame him?

And yet, just the thought of him continuing with his playboy ways made her feel sick to her stomach. She didn't want any other woman getting what he had given her. She didn't want him kissing other women like he'd kissed her. Didn't want him caressing, or holding, or teasing anyone but her.

Maybe, after their night together, he wouldn't want that either. Maybe he'd realize what she had.

They were a perfect match.

It was hilariously ironic when she thought about it. All this time, she'd been searching high and low for the right man for her and he'd been right under her nose.

"Give Holly Joy back to her daddy and mama, Noelle." Mimi's words pulled Noelle from her thoughts. "It's time we let Decker and Sweetie have Holly Joy to themselves."

Sweetie and Decker were lying together in the hospital bed, looking exhausted but happy. They looked even happier when Noelle gently nestled Holly Joy between them. It was a picture-perfect moment Noelle couldn't pass up. She pulled out her cellphone and snapped numerous pictures.

"Please don't be posting those on your social media, Elle," Sweetie said. "I look like hell."

Decker leaned over and kissed her cheek. "I think you look more beautiful than you have ever looked in your life, Sweets."

The loving comment made Noelle think about all the sweet things Casey had said to her the night before. Since being nice had never been her and Casey's relationship, she couldn't help having her doubts. Had he meant them or were they just part of his seduction? Words he said to all the women he'd had sex with?

The doubts continued circling around in her head as she helped Hallie and Jace gather up the stuffed animals and flowers the family had brought so Decker and Sweetie wouldn't have to worry about them when they left the hospital in the morning.

"Hallie and I will drop all this by Decker and Sweetie's," Jace said. "And we'll pick up the dogs from Melba too." Since Sweetie's labor had been so long, Melba had picked up Gilley and Buck from the bed-and-breakfast and Sweetie and Decker's dogs, George Strait and Dixie Chick, from their house and taken them home.

"Thanks, Jace." Sweetie glanced around. "Thank y'all for being here."

"No need to thank us," Mimi said. "That's what family does."

"Of course it is." Mama leaned over to give Holly a kiss on her head. "Liberty just texted and said she, Jesse, Belle, and Corbin will leave Austin right after the wedding and will be here in the morning to drive y'all home. And Cloe and Rome will be here tonight to see Holly Joy—after they drop off Autumn Grace at Holiday Ranch." Sweetie's labor had been so long Cloe hadn't been able to be there for the birth. Autumn Grace had made it very clear she didn't like being without her mama . . . and mama's milk.

Once everyone exchanged hugs and goodbyes, they filed out of the room. Noelle had held off calling Casey because she hadn't wanted her family listening in. But once in her car, she didn't hesitate to dial his number and was thoroughly disappointed when he didn't answer. His voicemail clicked on saying leave a message and she got a little flustered.

"Hey. It's me . . . your friendly neighborhood baker. I just wanted to call and tell you that Sweetie had a beautiful little girl. Holly Joy. So . . . that's awesome." She rolled her eyes at how stupid she was sounding. "Anyway, call me when you get a chance. I'm going home to get some sleep."

After being up for almost two days straight, she had no trouble falling asleep. It was dark by the time she woke up. She immediately reached for her cellphone to checked for texts or missed calls from Casey. She had numerous texts from the sister loop of Sweetie sending pictures of Holly Joy and her sisters exclaiming over them, but none from Casey. It was starting to annoy her. Why wasn't he texting or calling? Had something happened out at the ranch?

She quickly texted him. **Is everything okay at the ranch?**

It didn't take long for her to get an answer. Her phone pinged almost immediately with an incoming text.

I wouldn't know I'm not there.

Her heart beat faster as she imagined him standing on her front porch. She smiled as she texted him back. Exactly where are you?

Her phone pinged with a reply. **Hellhole.**

Her smile faded. He was at the Hellhole? What was he doing at the Hellhole? She started to text the question, but then decided she didn't want to come off as some clingy girlfriend. He'd probably just had dinner there and was having a couple beers with his friends. Casey had a lot of friends. Noelle should just tell him to stop by when he was on his way home.

That's what a confident woman would do.

Unfortunately, Noelle had never been confident where Casey was concerned.

An hour later, she was parking in the Hellhole's parking lot.

As always, Bobby Jay had gone all out for Christmas. The restaurant and bar was covered with strings of multicolored lights, and huge wreaths made out of beer cans hung on the doors. Inside, twinkle lights and garland hung along the walls and over the long bar. A tall artificial tree covered in mini cowboy hats, chili pepper lights, and loops of rope stood in the corner next to the stage. On the stage, a band wearing Santa caps over the crowns of their cowboy hats was playing a Morgan Wallen song.

While Noelle took in all the festive decorations, she kept an eye out for Casey. It didn't take long to find him. He stood at the bar with one of his friends . . . a female friend. Because men can have female friends—female friends who lean in and whisper in their ear. Friends whisper to each other all the time.

They just don't usually kiss them right on the lips.

Jealous shot through Noelle like it had been injected straight into her veins. She didn't hesitate to make her way over to the bar where Casey and his not-so-friendly friend were kissing. In his defense, Casey looked like he was trying to push the blonde away . . . until Noelle showed up. There was stunned surprise in those sea-blue orbs before they slammed shut and he tugged the blonde closer, deepening the kiss.

It was quite obvious what he was doing.

She crossed her arms. "You about finished making your point?"

He drew away from the blonde and turned to her. He did the innocent lip-biting thing that Noelle hated. "Point? What point would that be, Smelly Ellie?" His words weren't slurred, but they were spoken slowly and deliberately. The way people did when they'd had too much to drink. He nodded at the blonde tucked under his arm. "Do you know Sheila from Odessa? She's a lovely gal who likes tequila, Appaloosa horses, and delivers bread and cookies to grocery stores. And speaking of cookies . . . this is my girlfriend, Noelle Holiday, who smells like fresh-baked cookies because she's the best baker this side of the Pecos. Maybe one day you'll deliver her cookies."

Sheila turned to him. "Your girlfriend?"

Casey blinked. "Did I say girlfriend. I meant fake girlfriend. Strictly fake. Well, maybe not strictly." His smile slipped. "There was the other night when we weren't strictly at all. But then I found out that her mother broke both my mama's and daddy's hearts and I think one more

Remington heart being broken by a Holiday is one too many."

Noelle stared at him. "What are you talking about?" She glanced at the half-empty bottle of tequila on the bar. "How much have you had to drink?"

Before he could answer, Sheila jumped in. "Wait a second. You're Noelle Holiday from *Holiday Kitchen*?"

"That she is!" Casey said. "And I'm her cowboy hero . . . who hasn't had nearly enough to drink." He grabbed the bottle and poured himself a shot. He downed it with a quick backward jerk of his head. He went to grab the bottle again, but Noelle grabbed it first.

"You've had enough, Casey."

"She's right. You have had enough." Sheila grabbed the purse sitting on the bar. "And so have I. I'm not going to be the reason Noelle Holiday breaks things off with her cowboy hero."

When she was gone all the humor fell from Casey's face. "Go home, Ellie."

"I'm not going home until we talk."

He stared at her for a long moment before he took her arm and pulled her to the door. Once outside in the parking lot, he released her and flexed his hand as if it had been burned.

"You want to talk. So talk."

"I know what you're doing. You're trying to prove to yourself that last night wasn't special. That it didn't mean anything. But it *was* special, Casey. You know it and so do I."

She didn't know what she expected him to say,

but it wasn't what he said. "You're right. It was one of the best fucks I've ever had."

She slapped him so hard across the face that his head snapped back. When he looked at her, his smile was gone and his eyes were clearer.

He rubbed his jaw. "Good one, Ellie. I deserved that." He held out his arms. "In fact, you have every right to kick my ass." His arms fell back to his sides and a defeated look entered his eyes. "Unfortunately, it won't change the fact that you gave your blossom to the wrong guy. I'm no hero, Ellie. I'm more of an antihero. A pathetic loser who will fuck up your life if you don't stay away from me. So go on home to your loving mama and daddy and leave me to—"

She cut him off. "Wallow in your own self-pity?" She snorted. "I *should* kick your ass. I should kick your ass from one end of this town to the other. Because someone needs to knock some sense into you. I don't need a cowboy hero. All I need is a man who is willing to love me like I deserve to be loved. But you're right about one thing, that man isn't you. I get that you've had a hard life. Well, welcome to the world, Casey Remington! Lots of people have hard lives. Like you, I have a gruff daddy who struggled to show his love to his six daughters. Yes, I have a loving mama and grandma, but I also had five siblings I never felt like I could measure up to. But you don't see me giving up on love and life to sit on the whiny chair like a big-assed baby. I keep fighting for what I want—not to prove anything to them, but to prove something to myself. But you don't seem to want to prove anything to anyone except that you're a good-for-nothing cowboy who crawls from one bed to the other trying to replace the love you didn't get from your mama!"

Casey's eyes widened. "That's not why I get with women. And are you trying to say your life was just as hard as mine? The hell it was! Your daddy won. He found the woman he loved while my daddy married his second choice and ruined all our lives."

She stared at him. But before she could ask what he was talking about, Reid Mitchell stepped out of the bar. He glanced between them and Noelle realized they must look like two WWE wrestlers getting ready for a throw down.

"Is there a problem, Ms. Holiday?"

Casey answered before she could. "There's no problem. I was just leaving." He turned and headed for his truck. She knew he wouldn't turn back around. She knew he was walking away for good.

"You go ahead and run, Casey Remington!" she yelled after him. "You're right! You don't deserve me! I certainly don't want a man who can't even believe in himself!" He was in his truck and backing out, but she kept yelling. "In fact, I don't need any man! I can make it just fine on my own! I am woman, hear me roar!"

She actually made a pathetic roaring sound . . . which quickly turned into a choked sob as she watched Casey pull away.

A second later, she was crying like a whiny big-assed baby in Reid's arms.

Chapter Nineteen

After leaving the Hellhole, Casey went to a dive bar located just off the interstate where he drank even more and ended up getting in a fight with some big ol' bouncer wearing a Will Ferrell's *Elf* T-shirt who kicked his ass before tossing him out into the parking lot. He lay there with the asphalt biting into his cheek for a few minutes before he got up, limped to his truck, and passed out.

When he woke the next morning, he looked and felt like hell. But he wasn't ready to go home. He didn't know if he would ever be ready to go home. Not only because he was pissed off at his daddy for not mentioning he'd been in love with Darla Holiday, but also because he didn't want to run into Noelle. He felt like shit about how he'd treated her. She was right. He didn't deserve her. She deserved someone much better.

But if that were the case, why did he feel like someone had sucker punched his heart after leaving the Hellhole? Casey had heard every word she'd yelled at him and watched in the rearview mirror as Reid had pulled her into his arms to comfort her.

She had wanted a cowboy hero and she had gotten one.

Just not Casey.

He thumped the steering wheel. "Dammit, why couldn't it be me?"

A state patrol car drove past and slowed, the patrolman giving him a hard look. Casey figured it was time to go. He didn't have a location in mind until he'd been driving for an hour and saw a road sign with the mileage to Baton Rouge. Six hours later, he was standing on his mama's doorstep.

While Rome looked like their daddy, Casey looked more like their mama. They had the same blond hair. The same blue eyes. The same fake smile. A smile Glorieta pinned on as soon as she stepped into the gaudily decorated room the housekeeper had shown him to.

It wasn't the first time he'd been to the house. He'd come once before when he'd only been eighteen and looking for a mama. He hadn't found one then, and he didn't find one now. She treated him like a casual friend who had dropped by unannounced.

"Casey. How lovely of you to stop by." She breezed into the room wearing some kind of white loungewear and tons of gold jewelry. She froze when she got a good look at his face. Which must look pretty damn scary between the bruises and bloodshot eyes. Her eyes widened, but she recovered quickly. "Would you like something to drink . . . or perhaps a cold compress?"

"I'm good."

She nodded and held out a hand. "Please sit down."

"I can't stay." The relief on her face should have hurt, but he only felt a slight pinch of sadness and it was more for her. "Why did you leave Sam? Was it because he was in love with Darla Holiday?"

She stared at him with startled eyes and he thought he'd just put his foot in his mouth. Or a dagger through his mother's heart. Before he could feel too badly, she started to laugh. It was the first time he'd ever seen her laugh and he was shocked by how much it reminded him of Rome when he found something hilariously funny.

Casey didn't find it amusing. "So I guess that wasn't the reason."

Glorieta sobered and blotted at the corners of her eyes with a tissue she pulled from a gold tissue box. "No. It wasn't because your father was in love with Darla Holiday—or thought he was in love with Darla Holiday. In case, you don't know this about your daddy, he always wants what he can't have. I think he just wanted her because Hank did. Romantic love isn't something your daddy has time for. He cared about me, but I think he just saw me as a way to get children."

She hesitated. "He so wanted children. For all his faults, he loves you and Rome more than he loves anything in the world. Including that damn ranch. Which is why I didn't take y'all with me. I knew he could give you a better life than I could. I couldn't see two young boys being happy moving from a big ranch with horses and every other kind of animal to the small city apartment I lived in after leaving your father."

Casey wanted to point out that she hadn't lived in a small apartment for long. But he hadn't come to point fingers. He'd come . . . hell, he didn't know why he'd come. Maybe he was just hurting and wanted to see his mama. The truth hit him hard and he realized maybe Noelle was right. Maybe his carousing had never been about not wanting to end up heartbroken like his daddy. Maybe it had more to do with searching for his mama's love.

Or any woman's love.

"So you want to tell me what happened to your face?" she asked.

"I got drunk and needed to be taken down a peg or two."

She nodded, as if she understood all about getting drunk and needing to be taken down a peg, before she walked to the minibar. When she returned, she had a bottle of Perrier and ice wrapped up in a linen napkin. "Sit."

He glanced at the white sofa. "I don't want to get your couch dirt—"

"Sit." When he did, she handed him the bottle of water and gently pressed the ice to his cheek. "Was it over a girl?"

He sighed and nodded. "Noelle Holiday."

"Ahh." She handed him the ice and sat down next to him. "So you have conflicting feelings about falling for a Holiday like your daddy did and having your heart broken."

He wanted to deny it, but then realized he couldn't. Mainly, because his heart did feel broken. "I'm scared. I'm scared she'll figure out that I'm all smoke and mirrors."

"Smoke and mirrors?"

He ran a hand through his hair and tried to collect his thoughts. "Noelle is special. She has big dreams. Dreams of owning her own bakery and being a social media influencer. My dreams are much simpler. I'm a rancher. That's all I've ever wanted to be. Eventually she's going to realize that being a rancher's wife is not enough . . . I'm not enough."

Glorieta reached out and covered his hand with hers. "Of course you're enough."

He looked down at her fingers covered in gold and diamonds. "I wasn't enough to hold you."

When he glanced up, he saw that tears had filled her eyes. She quickly released his hand and got up, walking to the huge floor-to-ceiling front window.

He felt like shit for upsetting her.

"I'm sorry."

She sniffed and shook her head. "No, you have every right to feel that way. And I understand perfectly why you do. I felt the same way when my daddy left me."

Okay, this was news.

"Your daddy left you?"

She turned around and nodded, tears glistening in her eyes. "And instead of learning from it, I repeated the cycle. You'll never know how sorry I am for that, Casey. My daddy was the one who wasn't enough when he left. I was the one who wasn't enough when I left—or thought I wasn't enough all based on my daddy's leaving and on your father's inability to love me. But what I'm just starting to understand, after many years of therapy, is that I am enough. But only if I believe I am. Thinking you're not enough can lead you to make a lot of mistakes. I thought I wasn't enough as a daughter or a wife or a mother so I decided to stop trying to be those things—to just give up. But that's the biggest mistake you can make, Casey. To not believe in yourself and give up."

His mother's words were almost identical to Noelle's. *I certainly don't want a man who can't even believe in himself!* And that's exactly what Casey was. He was a man who didn't believe in himself. A man who thought he wasn't good enough to run a ranch as well as his brother and father. A man who thought he wasn't good enough to be a husband or a father. A man who thought he wasn't good enough to be loved.

"I guess like mother like son," he said.

His mama smiled. "You want the number of my therapist?"

His mama ended up talking him into staying for dinner. It turned out to be quite nice. The filet mignon was way too small to be considered a steak and the lobster bisque too rich, but he actually enjoyed talking with his mama and her husband, his stepfather. The last time he'd been there he'd been a resentful teen with a bone to pick. Which probably explained why his mama had been so wary when she greeted him this time.

Now that he wasn't as angry and belligerent, he discovered a different person from the arrogant, selfish mama he'd first met. This mama was a charismatic woman who hid her low self-esteem behind a smile and teasing blue eyes.

Just like he did.

After dinner, she talked him into staying the night. She showed him to a bedroom that looked like it belonged in a ritzy Vegas hotel. He took a long, hot shower. When he got out, he discovered his clothes and boots missing, satin pajamas on the foot of the bed, and bottles of water and aspirins on the nightstand.

Since he hadn't worn pajamas since he could remember, he climbed beneath the super-soft sheets naked. His body was exhausted, but his mind wasn't. It ran through everything that had happened in the last few days. There had been a lot. But what his mind zeroed in on was his night with Noelle. The moment when she had cradled his jaw in her soft hand and said, *You're enough, Casey. You're more than enough.*

She had flat told him he was enough for her and he still hadn't believed it. If he didn't want to end up like his mama—filled with regret and estranged from his kids—he needed to pull his head out and start believing in himself. Maybe he'd never be as good at ranching as his brother and his daddy, but that didn't matter. What mattered was enjoying the gift God had given him and giving it his best.

That went for Noelle too.

For whatever reason, God had seen fit to put her back in his life and he had ruined it. He had completely ruined it. All because he had let self-doubt and insecurities make him believe he'd end up like his daddy—a pitiful, lonely man staring at a picture of the woman he loved. But he didn't have to end up like his father. Or his mother. He had the ability to make his life whatever he wanted.

He wanted Noelle.

But what if it was too late? What if he had already lost her?

He quickly sat up and grabbed his cellphone from the charger he'd placed it in before he'd gotten into the shower. He wasn't going to call her. When he apologized, he wanted to do it face-to-face. But he did want to see if she'd broken up with him on social media. He released a relieved breath when he opened the social media site and saw Noelle hadn't posted in the last couple days. Maybe that meant he still had a chance.

Her last post was made the night of their rendezvous at the bed-and-breakfast. She was wearing the cherry dress she'd worn that night and curling her hair with a big-barreled curling iron. He tapped on the post and her voice came through his phone speaker, making his heart ache.

"Hey y'all! I know, I know, I should be in the kitchen whipping up my Grandma Mimi's favorite molasses cookies like I promised y'all yesterday. But some things take precedence over baking." Her green eyes sparkled. "Like love."

Casey's heart beat triple time at hearing the word *love* from those candy apple lips. He had the uncontrollable urge to lean in and kiss his phone and beg her to say the word again and again just for him.

Just for real.

But it wasn't real. It was all for her followers. Right?

He watched as she continued in a giddy voice that didn't sound fake at all.

"That's right. I'm gettin' all dolled up for Casey. We have a very special night planned and I have to admit I'm a little nervous. But I know when he pins those ocean-blue eyes on me, all my nerves will fade clean away. Casey has the ability to make a girl feel like she's the focus of his entire world." Her smile was soft and captivating. "Isn't that all any of us want? A man who makes us feel like we're special—like we're the other half of his heart." Her eyes widened. "Oops, I haven't been paying attention to the time. I need to go before I'm late for our date. But I'll talk to you soon and tell you all about it. Remember, there's always something cookin' in the *Holiday Kitchen*."

The video cut off, leaving Casey staring at her image.

His heart felt like it weighed about a thousand pounds. She was the entire focus of his world. She always had been. As a kid, he hadn't known how to deal with his feelings so he'd teased her. As an adult, he still didn't know how to deal with his feelings so he'd pushed her away.

He figured he had two choices.

He could continue to be an idiot and lose her.

Or he could prove to her that she was the other half of his heart and become her cowboy hero.

Chapter Twenty

Noelle would have spent the next few days sobbing in her pillow if Sheryl Ann hadn't caught the flu and asked her to run Nothin' But Muffins until she was feeling better. With Christmas being only a couple weeks away, the little café was hopping. So Noelle didn't have time for tears . . . until at night when she was tucked in bed, then she had a regular weep-fest—interspersed with cussing rage fits.

But during the day, she put on a bright smile and tried to act like everything was just peachy. She had always been good at acting. Or so she thought until all her sisters showed up at Nothin' But Muffins one afternoon.

"What happened?" Noelle asked. "Is Daddy okay? Mama? Mimi?"

"Don't overreact," Hallie said. "We're just having a Secret—" She cut off and glanced at Coach Denny, who was sitting at a nearby table eating a Sugarplum Fairy muffin. He stopped when he noticed all the sisters looking at him and quickly lowered the muffin and jumped to his feet.

"I should be going. Jace mentioned wanting to

go over some game film for next season and I wouldn't want to keep him waiting."

After he left, Belle flipped the front sign to *closed*.

Noelle's eyes widened. "What are you doing, Belly? I can't close for another three hours."

"We're having a quick Secret Sisterhood meeting. It won't take long because Sweetie and Cloe have to get back to those sweet babies."

"You mean Sweetie has to get back to her sweet baby." Hallie pulled out a chair and flopped down. "Autumn Grace isn't what I'd call sweet." She grinned. "She's more like her Auntie Hal."

Cloe took a chair at the table with Hallie. "Autumn Grace is too sweet . . . sometimes." She looked exhausted and Noelle felt badly she hadn't been able to help her sister the last few days. Not only because she was taking over for Sheryl Ann, but also because she couldn't chance seeing Casey. If she did, she didn't know if she'd start crying or take a rolling pin to his head.

Probably the rolling pin.

Liberty moved over to the muffin display case. "Nothing wrong with a female letting her needs be known." She pointed at the case. "Can you get me two Sugarplum Fairy muffins, Elle?"

Noelle took the muffins from the case and placed them in a box, along with a selection of other muffins she knew were her sisters' favorites. "So what is this meeting about?" She almost dropped the box when everyone spoke at the same time.

"You."

She glanced around. "Me? What about me?"

As president of their club, Sweetie fielded the question. "Mama told us that you've turned down the job offer of assistant pastry chef in Dallas."

"So?"

"So why would you do that?" Cloe asked. "We all thought you wanted to live in a big city and work under an experienced French pastry chef."

"Please don't tell us you've changed your mind again, Elle," Hallie said. "What do you want to be this time? An Olympic figure skater? An opera singer?"

Noelle scowled. "Very funny. No, I still want to bake. And just for the record, I've never wanted to live in a big city and work under an experienced pastry chef. I only applied because I thought it was the only way to get what I do want—my own bakery. But now I've decided to come up with another way to achieve that dream."

"Why?" Belle asked. "There must be a reason you want to stay here, Elle."

Liberty sighed. "Quit beating around the bush, Belly." She shot a glance at Noelle. "We want to know if your decision has something to do with Casey?"

Before Noelle could reply, Hallie did. "Talk about beating around the bush, Libby." She turned to Noelle. "We don't want to know anything. We already know that you went and did exactly what we feared you would. You've fallen for Casey just like you fell for all the other guys you've dated. And we all know that's why you turned down the job at that hotel and why you've been acting so weird lately. You've gotten it in that romantic head of yours that you and Casey are going to get married and live happily ever after. Well, wake up, Elle! Casey Remington is not the marrying kind."

Cloe smiled sadly. "I'm afraid she's right, Elle. I love Casey, but he has some relationship issues due to his mama leaving him." She hesitated. "And it's even worse now that he found out about Mama and Sam."

"Mama and Sam?" Hallie stared at Cloe. "What about Mama and Sam?"

Cloe glanced around at her sisters. "I guess Mama and Sam dated at one time. Which explains the feud between Daddy and Sam."

Noelle blinked. So that was what Casey had been talking about the other night at the Hellhole. "Mama and Sam dated? Like they were in love?"

Instead of Cloe answering, Sweetie did. "Mama thought she was in love with Sam, but then she fell for Daddy."

"You knew about it too?" Liberty spoke around a bite of muffin. "Why were the rest of us kept in the dark? Remember the entire sisters-don't-keep-secrets-from-sisters rule?"

Sweetie shrugged. "I'm sorry, but Mama asked me not to tell."

"But that was something that should have been shared," Hallie said. "It would have explained a lot about Daddy and Sam's feud. No wonder they don't like each other. They're both in love with the same woman."

"Having me marry Rome and move into his house must have been extremely hard for poor Sam," Cloe said.

Hallie snorted. "And now his other son has seduced Noelle. Obviously, Remingtons have a thing for Holidays."

Noelle finally snapped out of the stunned daze she'd been in. "Casey didn't seduce me! I'm the one who wanted to have sex with him." She looked at Cloe. "When did he find out about Sam and Mama?"

"The night Sweetie went into labor."

No wonder he'd been so cruel at the Hellhole. He'd been reeling from what he'd found out. Noelle knew how she would feel if she found out her daddy was in love with another woman. She'd be angry and want to place blame. Not only on her father, but the woman he'd been in love with . . . and her entire family.

"It doesn't matter who seduced who, Elle," Belle said. "Nor does it matter what happened between Sam and Mama decades ago. What matters is the present moment. We're here because we don't want to see you get hurt."

Too late. Noelle was already hurt and her sisters' lack of confidence in her was making her feel even more so.

Hallie jumped back in. "It's time to stop living in the fantasy world of social media and start living in the real world. In the real world, you were just offered a great job. So take it and quit mooning over a man who isn't—"

The door opened and Sunny swept in. "Hey,

y'all! Sorry, I'm late, but I had a little bit of a run-in with Reid Mitchell."

"A run-in?" Belle asked.

Sunny unwound the red scarf from around her neck and hung it on the coatrack by the door. "I wasn't looking where I was going and ran smack dab into him on my way down the street. And all I can say is the man is like a wall of pure muscle. Anyway, what did I miss? Fill me—" She cut off when her gaze shifted to the corner table next to the Christmas tree. "Hey, Ms. Stokes. I didn't realize you were part of the Secret Sisterhood."

All the sisters turned to find Mrs. Stokes sitting at the table, casually sipping herbal tea. Noelle had sold her that tea and a Sugarplum Fairy muffin, but that had been over an hour ago and she'd thought Mrs. Stokes had left. Probably because her ratty mink stole was decorated with so many Christmas broaches and pins, she looked like part of the tree. Noelle wondered how much of the conversation she'd overheard.

She didn't have long to wonder.

Ms. Stokes set her cup down. "No, I'm not part of the Secret Sisterhood, but I'll be happy to fill you in on the meeting. I believe the Holiday sisters were browbeating Noelle because she falls in love easily and has decided to turn down the job offer to work as a pastry chef in an overcrowded and polluted big city. They're worried she's going to get hurt by the dastardly playboy Casey Remington if she continues to stay here in Wilder." She looked at Sweetie. "Isn't that it in a nutshell, Madam President?"

Sweetie shot her sisters a stunned look before she cleared her throat and answered Mrs. Stokes. "Yes, ma'am."

"Then it's probably a good thing I'm not part of this club. Because if I were and you were getting into my business as much as you seem to be getting into Noelle's, I would have to tell y'all to go to hell in a handcart." She glanced at Noelle. "Because I'm a grown woman who can decide what job I want, what man I date, and where I choose to live. Because no one can live my life better than I can." She glanced around at all the sisters. "Which is why your mama didn't tell you about dating Sam. It was none of y'all's business." Her gaze returned to Noelle. "Love isn't always a choice. Usually it just sneaks up on you and grabs your heart before you even know it's happening. Sometimes, it works out—like your mama and daddy. And sometimes, it doesn't—like your mama and Sam. But that shouldn't stop anyone from trying to hold on to it with both hands. Now if you'll excuse me, I have a bank to run." She opened her purse and placed a ten-dollar tip on the table before heading for the door.

Sunny quickly held it open for her. "Nice to see you again, Ms. Stokes."

Mrs. Stokes snorted. "Tell that brother of yours that I've done what he asked so now he has to do what I asked. A bet is a bet." Then she swept out the door and was gone.

All the sisters released a groan. All the sisters, but Sunny and Noelle. Sunny looked thrilled Mrs. Stokes had been an honorary member of their club for a short time while Noelle was mulling over what the older woman had said. When her words finally sunk in, she realized Mrs. Stokes was one hundred percent right.

Noelle had spent all her life trying to win her sisters' respect, but now she realized in order to do that, she needed to stand her ground and live her life the way she saw fit.

She took a deep breath before she spoke. "I know y'all came here today because you love me and don't want to see me get hurt. But as Mrs. Stokes so eloquently pointed out, it's my life to live. Not yours. If I fall in love with Casey Remington and get my heart broken, that's my choice. I didn't try to stop you from falling for Jace, Hal. Even though he was Sweetie's ex and we had a Secret Sisterhood rule about dating exes. Or keep you from getting into an arranged marriage with Rome, Cloe. Or throw a fit when you hopped in bed with the villains taking our parents' ranch, Libby and Belly."

Her sisters all exchanged guilty looks as she continued. "I get I'm your baby sister. I'll always be your baby sister. But I'm also an adult. An adult who graduated top of my culinary school and has over fifty thousand social media followers—not just because I'm dating a cowboy hero, but because I'm a damn good baker. Yes, I might be dramatic and emotional and fall in love at the drop of a hat, but there's not a damn thing wrong with that. Nor is there a damn thing wrong with me changing my mind about taking the job in Dallas. I don't want to live in Dallas. I want to live here with my annoying big sisters who always want to tell me what to do and what to think and what big mistakes I'm making."

She strode over and flipped the closed sign to open. "Now if you'll excuse me, I have muffins to make." She turned around and headed into the kitchen. As she started another batch of Sugarplum Fairy muffins, she could hear her sisters' whispered arguing. A few minutes later, they all filed into the kitchen.

"We're sorry," Sweetie said. "You're right. You are an adult who can make her own choices." She smiled. "And you should tell your sisters to go to hell in a handcart when they need to be reminded of that. But you will always be our baby sister and we'll always want to protect you . . . even if you don't need protecting."

Noelle sighed. "I know, but sometimes I'd like to know that I'm not just a silly kid sister who keeps screwing things up."

"Keeps screwing things up?" Belle stared at her. "How have you screwed up?"

"Boys. Careers. You name it."

"You didn't screw up," Sweetie said. "You just keep trying things until you figure out what you want. Which is better than me. I wasted years of my life because I stubbornly refused to give up on becoming a country singer even when I hated it."

"And once you figured out what you wanted to do, Elle," Liberty said. "You stuck with it and become a social media baking influencer."

Noelle glanced at Hallie. "Which some people still think is stupid."

Hallie sighed. "Okay, so I don't get it, but that doesn't mean it's stupid, Elle. I watched some of your posts and . . . well, I can see why people follow you. You're not just a great baker, you're also good at making people feel comfortable and loved. You always have been good at that. And maybe I'm a little jealous. You give of yourself so freely and I've never been able to do that."

"It's true, Elle," Sunny said. "People love you because you give love. You've certainly made me feel loved and part of the family."

"You are a giver," Cloe agreed. "What you've done for me and all the Remingtons in the last few weeks is a perfect example. You filled our home with Noelle cheer."

"Noelle cheer." Belle smiled. "That's the perfect way to describe you, Elle. You bring cheer to everyone. Your family. Your followers. And everyone you meet. If we made you feel less than, we're sorry."

She couldn't stop the tears welling up in her eyes. "Y'all" was all she got out before her sisters surrounded her in a sister huddle hug. When she noticed Sunny holding back, she waved her over. "Get in here. You're part of this now." Sunny smiled brightly and quickly joined the huddle. There were tears and smiles and lots of sisterly loving looks. Being cocooned in that much love made the truth pop right out of Noelle's mouth.

"I love Casey Remington!"

Hallie's eyes bugged out and she opened her mouth to say something—no doubt "I knew it!"—but Sweetie cut her off.

"Elle's a big girl, Hal. She can deal with it." She gave Noelle a hug. "Now I'm going to get my sweet angel from Mama."

"I need to get back to my sweet angel too." Cloe smiled. "Or my sweet hellion." She gave Noelle a hug. "For what it's worth, Casey hasn't been acting like himself the last few days. So maybe . . ."

Noelle shook her head. "He doesn't, but thanks for trying to make me feel better. And Sweetie's right. I'll deal with it."

"Of course you will." Liberty hugged her. "You're a Holiday."

"If you need us," Belle said as she pulled her close. "We're here for you."

"Always." Hallie roughly thumped her back.

Once everyone left, Noelle blew her nose, washed her hands, and got back to work. Customers kept arriving and she was exhausted by closing time, but there was one more thing she needed to do before she went home.

It didn't take her long to set up for her post. She put on her favorite holly apron and her crimson-red lip stain and matching gloss. She wished she had some eye drops for her bloodshot eyes, but maybe it was a good thing she didn't. Maybe her followers needed to know Noelle Holiday cries sometimes.

She also fibs.

If her followers couldn't deal with that, then they were welcome to unfollow her. She was who she was and people could like her or not. She liked herself and that was all that mattered.

"Hey, y'all." She didn't give her usual smile because this wasn't a smiling kind of post. "So I have a confession to make." Her heart was pounding so loudly in her ears she thought she might be having a heart attack. She took a deep breath and powered through. "You see . . . well, the night that Casey showed up and saved me. It wasn't exactly how it seemed. He did save me. That part is true. And we have known each other since kindergarten. That's true too."

The bell on the front door rang.

Darn it! She'd forgotten to lock up again. But maybe a customer was a blessing in disguise. Now she would have to cut the post short and wouldn't have time for a lot of painful questions.

"As you heard, that was a customer. So I can't talk long. But I just needed to tell you that I lied. Casey never brought me flowers or took me on a date or did any of the romantic things I said he did. Because he wasn't ever my real—"

"Sorry I'm late, Sugar Muffin."

Noelle whirled around to see Casey standing in the doorway, holding the biggest bouquet of red roses she'd ever seen in her life. There had to be a hundred. He strode over and handed her the huge bouquet before he leaned down and kissed her right on the lips. And it wasn't a little kiss. It was a long, breath-taking, body-frying, panty-sizzling kiss that left Noelle feeling like a pool of perfectly tempered chocolate . . . for all of two seconds.

Once the two seconds were up, she jumped to her feet and clocked him right over the head with the huge bouquet, sending red petals raining.

"Just what do you think you're doing, Casey Remington? You can't walk in here and kiss me as if nothing has happened. As if you haven't been the biggest jerk to ever walk the face of the earth!"

He pulled off his hat that was covered in red petals. His blue eyes held regret . . . along with plenty of fear.

"I know. I shouldn't have kissed you. You just looked so beautiful sitting there in my favorite apron with my favorite lipstick on my favorite lips. And I've just missed you so much that I couldn't help myself. And you're right. I *am* the biggest jerk to walk the face of the earth . . . although I would say I was more of an insecure, terrified idiot. You're also right that a man who doesn't believe in himself doesn't deserve you. Which is why I spent so many years acting like you weren't the girl I've always wanted—because I didn't think I was good enough for you. But dammit, Ellie, I'm done pretending. You're the only girl I want. You'll always be the only girl I want. And maybe I'm not good enough for you right now. But I'm gonna be. I'm gonna work my butt off proving to you that I'm worthy of your love. I'm gonna bring you loads of red roses and ask you out on dates and bake sugar cookies with you, until you finally realize I'm the man for you. No one else, Ellie."

He slapped his chest with his hat. "Me. I'm

your cowboy hero. I promise you I'm gonna be the best damn cowboy hero you could ever want or need. And if you have a problem with that, well, I'm sorry. Just like I couldn't stop teasing you, I'm not gonna stop loving you. Not now and not ever. So you just need to come to terms with the fact that you're stuck with me. You can beat me with roses or a rolling pin and tell me to go straight to hell, but I'm not going anywhere. And when you're ready to stop being mad at me and forgive me, I'm going to get down on one knee and ask you to spend the rest of your life with me." He smiled and his dimple winked. "Because Ellie Holiday and Casey Remington belong together and always have."

Noelle tried. She really tried. But she had never been good at keeping her emotions inside.

She burst into tears.

Casey pulled her into his arms. She didn't resist. Because he *was* her cowboy hero and always would be. "I'm sorry, baby. I'm so sorry. Please don't cry."

She socked his chest. "Just so you know, I'll never stop crying. I cry when I'm sad and I cry when I'm mad and I cry when I'm happy."

"And which one are you now?"

She smiled against his hard chest. "Happy. About as happy as a girl can get." She drew back and sniffed. "But that doesn't mean you're forgiven. You have a lot of kissing up to do before I will even think about accepting your marriage proposal. And just like with the other agreements we've made, there will need to be some rules.

Firstly, when I am ready for that marriage proposal, I'll expect the works. Candlelight dinner, maybe a string quartet playing our song—which we'll need to figure out—and the perfect engagement ring I'll help you pick out because you don't know a thing about what a woman wants."

He looked down at her with his pretty sea-blue eyes twinkling. "Oh, I think I know what a woman wants and I'll be happy to give it to you. But first I'd like to add a few rules to this agreement." He drew her closer. "There *will* be plenty of cuddling. Not just for one night, but for all the rest of our nights." He kissed her, a sweet, sultry kiss that ended much too soon. She went to chase his lips, but he shook his head. "There's one more rule. No posting on our time." He released her and leaned down to her phone so his handsome face filled the screen. "Sorry, folks, but some things that are cookin' in the *Holiday Kitchen* are private." He winked before he tapped the button to end the post.

He straightened and pulled her back into his arms. "Now where were we?"

She unsnapped a snap of his western shirt. "I believe you were about to give me what a woman wants."

He did.

Chapter Twenty-One

ONE THING ABOUT Noelle, once she decided what she wanted, she didn't waste any time getting it.

Casey loved that about her.

Especially when it turned out she wanted him.

It only took three dates and a buttload of red roses before she took him ring shopping, had him make a dinner reservation at the most expensive restaurant in Austin, and told him what string quartet to hire and the song they should play—what else? "The First Noel." He had to admit the evening turned out real nice. Even when Noelle cried through the entire dinner and really sobbed when she saw the huge diamond ring she'd picked out.

But that was his Ellie. She wore her emotions right there for everyone to see. Like now, when tears were streaming down her face with every word she spoke.

"I, Noelle Carol Holiday, take you, Casey Michael Remington, to be my lawfully wedded husband, to have and to hold from this day forward, for better, for worse, in sickness and in health, to love and to cherish, until death—" Her stubborn chin lifted as tears traced down her cheeks. "No, not even death is going to keep me from you, Casey Remington. We're fated to be together and I'm not letting you go for all eternity."

Casey grinned. "Anything you say ... wife." He didn't wait for the preacher to pronounce them husband and wife. He kissed her. She threw her arms around him and kissed him back.

All the townsfolk squeezed into the Remington barn for the wedding ceremony cheered and whistled their approval. Or maybe they were just glad he was cutting things short so they could all go home and get ready for Santa to come.

Noelle had insisted on getting married on Christmas Eve in the Remingtons' barn—but only after it had been painted the same bright red as the Holidays' barn and Casey and Rome had hung a huge Christmas wreath over the hayloft. Casey had added a *Happy Birthday, Noelle* banner. He wanted the wedding reception to be her first real birthday party so mixed in with the wedding gifts were also birthday gifts from her friends and family.

Just not from Casey.

His birthday gift would come later ... after they celebrated a union that had been fated since kindergarten.

Since Noelle was a chef, Casey had thought she'd want to plan and help prepare the entire reception dinner. But instead, she'd wanted a potluck because she said that every person in town had a specialty food she and Casey had grown up with and loved. It only made sense that they'd celebrate with all those fond food memories.

The variety of food from barbecue chicken wings to tuna casserole did bring back memories of Casey's childhood. But the thing that brought back the most memories was his new bride. Every time he looked at her, hundreds of images crowded his brain. Most were good, but there were a few bad ones. He figured that was all part of loving someone.

There were good times and bad times in every relationship.

His relationships with his parents were perfect examples. If he focused only on the bad, he'd never have a relationship with either one of them. So he'd decided to focus on the good and it seemed to be making things better between him and his mama and daddy.

He no longer tried to get under Sam's skin by playing the uncaring playboy. Before he asked Noelle to be his wife, he'd invited Hank over to the house to ask both his and Sam's permission to marry Noelle. Sam had looked more than a little blindsided to be sitting in his study with his archenemy—and that Casey was asking his permission about anything. He looked even more surprised when Casey started talking about the improvements he wanted to make to the ranch. After Hank left, Casey had started to go to bed when Sam had stopped him.

"I'm happy you have a plan, son. All I've ever wanted was your happiness."

With those words, Casey realized his father might not outwardly show his love, but it was there. It had always been there. And that was all that mattered.

The same went for Casey's mama.

Although Glorieta was getting better at outward displays of love. Before the wedding ceremony, she had fussed over him and Rome—fixing their hair and making sure their red bowties were straight. At the reception, she had hugged Cloe and Noelle and told them how happy she was to have them in the family and oohed and ahhed over Autumn Grace.

The Remingtons weren't a perfect family. But that was okay. Casey was learning that all families came with their own problems. Even the Holidays. And one of the biggest problems of being in the Holiday family was getting alone time with his wife. If Noelle wasn't line dancing with her sisters, she was two-stepping with her brothers-in-law or her daddy. Or helping her mama get out the desserts. Or sipping homemade elderberry wine with Mimi and Sunny.

Which is where Casey finally found her.

"We were just talking about you, Casey Remington." Mimi poured him a glass of wine and handed it to him. He had learned at their engagement celebration, after falling into the Holidays' Christmas tree and knocking it over, that Mimi's wine was potent. So he only took a small sip before he flashed the older woman a wink.

"I hope it was all good."

Mimi winked back. "What fun is a man who's

all good? Bad boys make much better husbands—something my granddaughter was smart enough to figure out on her own. Sunshine and I didn't even have to implement our plan."

Noelle glanced between the two women. "You and Sunny had a plan to get me and Casey together?"

Sunny jumped in. "Don't get mad, Elle. Mimi just thought that if I acted like I was interested in Casey, you'd realize you didn't hate him." She smiled brightly. "But as luck would have it, Casey showed up at Nothin' But Muffins and became your cowboy hero."

"Not luck," Mimi said. "Divine intervention. God has always had a plan for these two. And speaking of God's plans, we need to get to cuttin' that cake."

"Oh!" Noelle set down her glass of wine. "You're right, Mimi."

The wedding cake had been made by Noelle. The six-tiered Sugarplum Fairy cake with whole sugared plums shimmering on each white-iced layer was the prettiest cake Casey had ever seen in his life. But the best part was the cake topper: a grinning cowboy holding the end of a lasso wrapped around a dark-haired baker in a white chef's hat and holly-print apron.

Although the baker should be the one with the lasso.

Noelle had certainly lassoed Casey's heart.

And he never wanted her to let go.

After he and Noelle cut the Sugarplum Fairy cake and fed it to each other—or more like shoved it into each other's faces until they laughed so hard Noelle started crying—Casey thought they would move on to tossing the garter and bouquet. But instead, Noelle motioned to Liberty and Belle to join them and then watched with a soft smile on her face as Belle cut into the smaller cake sitting next to the wedding cake.

Casey had noticed the cake. He'd just thought it was extra in case they ran out. Now he realized it was decorated like the Fourth of July with red, white, and blue icing and sparkly stars. Once Belle had placed two slices on plates, she and Liberty handed the plates to their husbands. Jesse and Corbin looked as confused as Casey.

"Well, don't just stand there," Noelle said. "Try it."

Corbin cut into his slice first. Or tried to. "Umm . . . there's something in here."

"There's something in mine too." Jesse pushed back the cake and frosting with his fork to reveal a long stick of what looked like white chocolate. "What is this?" He lifted the stick that had two skinny pink lines painted across it. The townswomen gathered around seemed to figure it out right away and started sighing and whispering happily to each other.

The men seemed more stumped.

They all continued to stare at the white chocolate stick until Mrs. Stokes finally spoke.

"Oh, for the love of Pete! It's supposed to be a pregnancy test. Jesse and Corbin, your wives are obviously trying to tell y'all that you're gonna be daddies."

"A daddy?" Corbin looked at Belle. When she nodded with a trembling smile, he set down his plate, scooped her into his arms, and carried her straight to the ladder that led to the hayloft.

Jesse was still looking stunned. "But I thought . . ."

Tears traced down Liberty's cheeks. "I thought so too, but I guess God had other plans. Now are you just gonna stand there, Jesse Cates, or are you gonna—"

Jesse leaned his head back and released a war whoop that rang through the rafters before he dropped the fake pregnancy test and his plate of cake and swung his wife around in a circle while she laughed and everyone applauded.

Once the baby surprise was over, it was time to toss the garter and bouquet. Casey threw the garter too far and it bypassed the group of single men and ended up getting lost among the people standing around watching. But the bouquet was caught by Sunny. No doubt because Noelle aimed straight for her.

As Sunny was celebrating her good fortune, Casey took his bride's hand and led her out the barn door.

Noelle didn't ask any questions. She just cuddled his arm and smiled up at him with eyes that reflected the outdoor Christmas lights as he led her to his truck that had been decorated with more lights and a big sign in the back window that read, *#thebakerandthecowboyheroforever.*

Noelle sighed. "Forever and ever."

On the way into town, they sang Christmas

carols at the top of their lungs. They were singing about dashing through the snow when Casey bypassed the turnoff to the Holiday Bed and Breakfast where they planned to spend the night.

Noelle cut off singing. "You missed the turnoff, Case."

"So I did."

She turned to him. "What are you up to, Casey Remington?"

He bit his bottom lip and sent her his most innocent look. "Not a thing, Noelle Remington. Not a thing."

When he pulled into a parking space in front of Nothin' But Muffins, she became even more confused. "What are you doin', Case? It's closed. Sheryl Ann was at the wedding, remember?"

"Your sisters had their surprise and now it's time for yours." He hopped out and came around to open her door.

As soon as she got out, she hooked her arms over his shoulders. "You loving me is the best surprise a girl could ask for."

His heart swelled and he brushed a kiss over her cherry-red lips. "That shouldn't have been a surprise. I think I've loved you since you skipped into kindergarten in that rainbow tutu and big glittery bow. You looked like a pretty wrapped present I wanted just for me."

"Well, you got me. So why don't you take me back to the Noelle Room and do some unwrapping?"

"Oh, I plan to, honey. But first, your birthday

surprise. Although, just to warn you, it might not be as exciting as hitting one hundred thousand followers and getting that butter company to pay you to only use their butter in all your social media baking."

"That was a nice surprise, but I've learned that it doesn't matter how many sponsors, followers, or likes I get as long as I have my family's . . ." she leaned up and kissed him, ". . . and my sweet cowboy hero's love."

He smiled. "You'll always have that, Ellie." He released her and took her hand. "Now quit distracting me and come on." He led her to the door of the café.

"We can't get in, Case. I didn't bring my key."

He pulled a key out of his jeans pocket. "I just so happen to have one on me." He unlocked the door, and then held it open for her. When she stepped inside, her gaze immediately went to the sign surrounded by twinkle lights he'd hung that morning.

She read the words in an awed whisper. "Nothin' But Muffins, Sheryl Ann Starr and Noelle Holiday Remington, proprietors?" She turned to him in question and he smiled a smile straight from his heart. A heart this woman had claimed as her own.

"Sheryl Ann approached me a few weeks ago with the idea. I guess Mrs. Stokes suggested it when Sheryl mentioned how overwhelmed she felt dealing with all her family's issues. Mrs. Stokes convinced her that having a talented pastry chef as her partner would lighten her workload and give her someone to hand the café off to when she's ready to retire. But if you're not interested—"

Noelle cut him off. "Casey!" She flung her arms around him and hugged him tight before she drew back and pulled out her phone. "I have to tell Mama, Daddy, Mimi, and my sisters—and my followers! They're going to be as thrilled as I am."

He took her cellphone and slipped it in his back pocket. "Later. Right now . . ." He locked the door and turned to her with a wicked grin. "I have a naughty baker's fantasy I'd like to fulfill."

"A naughty baker's fantasy? And just what does that entail?"

He kissed the tip of her cute nose. "You're a smart woman, Noelle Holiday Remington, I think you can figure it out."

He took her hand and led her to the back where they ended up baking a little something of their own in the *Holiday Kitchen*.

THE END

Turn the page for a SNEAK PEEK of Katie Lane's next Holiday Ranch romance!

Sneak Peek!
Wrangling a Wild Texan

Chapter One

HYDROPLANING HAD ALWAYS sounded like a thrilling activity. Like parasailing. Or kite surfing. Or hang gliding. And there was nothing Sunshine Brook Whitlock loved more than a good thrill. She enjoyed walking on the wild side and was up for almost anything: cliff jumping, skydiving, and swimming with sharks. The more daredevil, the more she wanted to try it.

But as her Subaru spun out of control on the icy rain-slick highway, Sunny didn't feel the adrenaline rush of excitement that came with those other thrill-seeking pursuits. She felt the terrifying reality that these could be her last few seconds on the planet earth.

And seconds weren't nearly enough time to make up for twenty-four years of orneriness.

She might look like the perfect little ray of sunshine, but beneath her sweet smile and innocent brown eyes was a devious devil who had completely hoodwinked her two brothers . . . and everyone else. Mischievous activities drew her like a bee to honey. Over the years, she had become an expert at not getting caught. But now the jig was up and she'd have to face the heavenly jury. With her record, there was no way she was getting past those pearly white gates.

Which meant she was headed straight to—

"Hell!" she yelled as her car careened off the highway. A second later, it slammed into a fence post with a jarring impact that had her body jerking forward.

This was it. She was about to pay for her impulsive, irresponsible behavior. Unfortunately, her brothers would have to pay too. Corbin who had loved and spoiled her all her life. And Jesse who loved her just as much, even though they had met only a few months earlier. They would both be devastated by her untimely death. That upset her even more than spending the rest of her days as a deep-fried, spicy chicken wing.

But just as she resigned herself to The End of her life story, her seatbelt tightened and the airbag deployed, keeping her from flying through the rain-splattered windshield. She sat there for a stunned moment with her lungs pumping and her heart thumping before she glanced out at the miles of cattle-grazing pasture capped by stormy gray skies.

"I'm alive!" she yelled at the top of her lungs. "I'm alive!" She looked up at the roof of her car. "Thank you, thank you, thank you. I promise to do better and go to church every—"

"Sunshine Whitlock."

She startled at the authoritative female voice that echoed through the interior of her car. She swallowed hard. Obviously, God wasn't buying her oath. While she quivered with reverent fear, she also felt vindicated. She'd always suspected God was a woman.

"This is vehicle assistance. We were notified that your airbags deployed. Are you okay?"

"Oh!" She laughed with relief. "Yes, I'm fine, but you might want to send—" Before she could finish there was a frantic tapping on her side window. She turned to see a completely drenched and hysterical teenage girl.

"Oh my God!" Sophie Mitchell's muffled voice came through the glass. "Are you okay? I'm so sorry. I only glanced at my phone for a second. Just a second. I didn't mean to swerve into your lane. I'm so sorry ... so, so sorry." She covered her face with her hands and started sobbing.

Sunny quickly rolled down the window. "Hey, now. I'm fine, honey. Just fine. Are you okay?"

Sophie lowered her hands. The few times Sunny had been around the teenager, she'd noticed Sophie had a heavy hand with makeup. Between the rain and crying, most of that makeup was dripping down her face. Which made Sunny want to hand her a tissue ... and give her a quick tutorial on makeup application.

"I'm okay," Sophie sniffed. "But I won't be for long. My uncle is going to kill me. Kill me!"

Just the mention of Sophie's uncle had an image popping into Sunny's head. An image of a man with hair the color of a moonless night and intense eyes the color of expensive French champagne. Those features were accompanied by a movie star handsome face and hard, muscled body that would send any woman racing for her vibrator. Sunny had gone through numerous AA batteries fantasizing about Sophie's uncle.

Of course, in her fantasies, he was nice.

In real life, he was a grumpy bumpkin.

"Ms. Whitlock?" The vehicle assistance woman cut into Sunny's thoughts. "Do we need to send emergency assistance?"

Since the front of her car looked to be wrapped around a fencepost and her engine was making a weird whining noise, emergency assistance was definitely needed. But before she could confirm that, she glanced at Sophie and saw the pleading look in her amber eyes.

It was hard not to sympathize with the girl. All this sweet teenager had was a mean ol' uncle who acted like he'd rather be doing anything than being the guardian of his fifteen-year-old niece. Sunny didn't know the full story of why Sophie was living with her uncle. But she did know what it felt like to be dumped on some relative who didn't really want you. She and Corbin had been dumped more times than she could count. While she was good at not getting caught, a couple of those guardians *had* caught her and it hadn't been good. She refused to be the one responsible for getting Sophie punished.

She gave her an encouraging smile before she answered the vehicle assistance operator.

"No need to send help. It's just a little fender bender, something I can turn into my insurance. The sheriff doesn't need to come out in this kind of weather for no good reason." Especially when

Sheriff Decker Carson was married to one of the Holiday sisters and word would quickly get back to Corbin. While Corbin was a loving brother, he had a tendency to overreact. He would not be happy Sunny had driven from Houston to Wilder in an ice storm—especially when he had informed her of the impending storm and told her not to come until the following day.

But some things were worth braving a storm.

Like loyalty to the Sisterhood.

Tonight, the Holiday Secret Sisterhood was having a meeting and Sunny had spent her entire life wanting a sister. After Corbin and Jesse had married the Holiday twins, Sunny now had six. Six sisters to drink Mimi's homemade elderberry wine with and skinny dip at Cooper Springs with and confide her deepest, darkest secrets to. Not that she had confided her deepest, darkest secrets yet. But she hoped to. She hoped sisters would understand her wild side better than her brothers did.

"Let us know if you do need help," the vehicle assistance operator said.

"Will do!"

Once she hung up, Sunny turned to Sophie. "Well, you better get in so we can collaborate our stories."

Sophie didn't do much collaborating. She sat in the passenger seat and shivered while Sunny give her a stern lecture on the dangers of texting while driving and then made her give her solemn oath that she'd never do it again. Sophie was emphatically promising she wouldn't when

Sunny glanced out the windshield and noticed a dark blob heading toward them across the rain-soaked pasture.

As it drew closer, she saw it was a horse and rider. Since they were on Holiday Ranch land, it could be any number of people. Hank Holiday, the patriarch of the Holiday family. Darla, his wife. Mimi, his mama. One of the six Holiday sisters. Or one of the sisters' husbands—Sunny's brothers included.

But it wasn't any of those people.

Instead, it was the assistant ranch manager and Sophie's uncle.

"Oh, shit! That's Uncle Reid." Sophie turned to Sunny. "Please don't tell him about me texting and driving. He'll be mad enough that I took his truck without permission. If he finds out I ran you off the road, he'll put me on restriction for life."

Sunny stared at her. "You took his truck without permission?"

Sophie sputtered. "U-U-Uhh . . . I wasn't planning on being gone long. I was just gonna practice driving before the storm hit."

"Practice driving? You don't have your driver's license?"

"Well, no, but that's not my fault. In order to get my license, I need to have a ton of driving hours with a licensed driver and Uncle Reid just doesn't have the time. So I've been—"

"Driving by yourself and forging his name." Damn, this teenage girl reminded Sunny of herself. She'd forged her guardians' names on more than one occasion. But that didn't make it right. She blew out her breath. "Your uncle should put you on restriction for the rest of your life. That way you might stay alive."

"So you're gonna tell him?"

Sunny glanced out the window. The rain had slowed to more of a steady drizzle and she had no problem seeing Reid Mitchell clearly as he rode up on the beautiful chestnut horse. He looked like he belonged in an old western ... or a girl's wet dream. His rain-dripping Stetson was pulled low and he wore a long duster that flapped around his muscled legs as he effortlessly swung down from the horse. He turned in the direction of his truck that was parked on the side of the road a few yards away before his head swiveled to them. Sunny couldn't see his face, but she could feel the intensity of his gaze. He headed toward them in long ground-eating strides. When he pulled open Sophie's door, his golden eyes were filled with concern.

"Soph! Are you okay? Are you hurt?"

"I'm fine, Uncle Reid."

His gaze snapped over to Sunny and she experienced the same feeling she always experienced when he looked at her—like she was standing on a high cliff getting ready to jump ... or sitting in front of a really hot principal who was about to discipline her. "Are you hurt, Ms. Whitlock?"

She pushed down her naughty-girl principal fantasies and held out her arms. "Right as rain."

His gaze swept over her and her breathlessness grew. "So what happened?"

Sophie sent her a pleading look. As much as the teenager deserved to get into a whole mess of trouble, Sunny couldn't bring herself to tattle. It wasn't like teenagers didn't do stupid things. Sunny had stolen more than one car, driven without a driver's license, and texted while driving. So she couldn't very well point fingers.

She pinned on a bright smile. "What happened was I got a little too big for my britches and thought I could drive much faster on a slick highway than I could." That much was true. She had been going a little too fast on the slick blacktop. Of course, the truck coming straight at her hadn't helped. "I hydroplaned and ran off the road. Sophie stopped to make sure I was okay."

The concerned look left Reid's eyes to be replaced with an emotion that was easy to read: Annoyance. And people being annoyed with her was not something Sunny was used to. People loved her. Or if not loved her, at least liked her. And why wouldn't they? She was the life of every party. The beacon of light on the darkest days. The sweet little ol' gal who made people smile. In fact, making people smile was what she did best.

Just not with Reid Mitchell.

His face seemed to be frozen in a perpetual frown whenever she was around. No matter how bright and funny she was he always looked at her like she was an annoying pest he had repeatedly tried to exterminate without luck.

Today was no exception.

"Your recklessness could have killed someone," he snapped. "Like Sophie."

"No, Uncle Reid," Sophie jumped in. "Sunny was nowhere close to hitting me. She only skidded a little and I braked fast so I wouldn't hit her."

"But she could have hit you." He returned his attention to Sunny, his golden eyes glittering with anger. The breathless, tummy-knotting feeling he evoked grew until she thought she might pass out.

"Does your car run?"

His question made Sunny realize that her engine had quit. She turned the key to restart it and there was a loud grinding noise like a forgotten spoon in a garbage disposal. She turned it off and looked at the grumpy cowboy.

"I guess that would be a no."

His lips pressed into a firm line. "Get in the truck. I'll drive you to Corbin and Belle's house. I'm assuming that's where you were headed."

"Yes. But you don't need to drive me. I can walk. It's not that far."

He snorted. "I'm sure my boss would love to hear that I let his sister walk home in a rainstorm. Now grab your stuff and get in the truck. You too, Soph."

Sunny had never let men tell her what to do—even her two brothers. For a moment, she considered telling him to go to hell. But then he took off his rain slicker and held it out for Sophie. Sunny didn't know it if was the sweet way he enfolded his niece in the coat or the way the rain turned his white T-shirt transparent that made her follow his orders.

Probably the wet T-shirt.

Not even being pelted by cold, icy rain as she got out of the car could get the image of all those muscles out of her head. As she was opening her trunk to get her suitcase, he showed back up, holding the duster over both their heads to block the rain.

His white T-shirt was now no more than wet tissue paper. She should look away, but damned if she could. With his arms raised to hold the duster, he looked like a posing contestant in a body-building competition. His biceps were pumped into huge fist-sized knots, his pectorals flexed into tight nippled-slabs, and his stomach was a landscape of flat hardness bookended by tempting hipbones peeking above the waistband of his low-riding jeans.

And speaking of jeans, her eyes widened when she noticed the impressive bulge outlined by his wet wranglers.

"Stop."

At the gruff command, Sunny's gaze snapped up to find Reid's eyes narrowed in anger.

She lifted her eyebrows. "Stop what?"

"You know what, Ms. Whitlock. That innocent act isn't going to work with me. I know your type."

"Really? Exactly what is my type?"

He started to say something, but then closed his mouth and shook his head. "Never mind." Lowering the duster, he grabbed her suitcase from the trunk and turned to leave. Unwilling to let him brush her off so easily, she grabbed his arm to stop him.

It was like grabbing onto a bolt of lightning. An electric current raced through her, starting at the muscled forearm her fingers curled around and ending at the tip of her cowboy boots and the top of her wet head. She would have thought she was the only one who felt it if his breath hadn't sucked in and his pupils hadn't dilated. Before she could get over her reaction—and his—he jerked away.

"I think I need to make things perfectly clear, Ms. Whitlock. I'm not interested. Do you understand me? Not only because you're my boss's little sister and I don't want to get fired, but also because you're trouble. Trouble is the last thing I need right now. So stay away from me . . . and Sophie." He turned and headed to his truck, carelessly tossing her suitcase into the bed.

Any other woman would have felt embarrassed. Or annoyed. Or angry. Sunny felt none of those things. As she stood there in the cold drizzle and watched him climb into the cab of his truck and slam the door hard, she only felt one thing.

Challenged.

And Sunshine Brook Whitlock had never been able to ignore a challenge in her life.

Order
WRANGLING A WILD TEXAN Today!

https://katielanebooks.com/wrangling-a-wild-texan

Also by Katie Lane

Be sure to check out all of Katie Lane's novels!
www.katielanebooks.com

Holiday Ranch Series
Wrangling a Texas Sweetheart
Wrangling a Lucky Cowboy
Wrangling a Texas Firecracker
Wrangling a Hot Summer Cowboy
Wrangling a Texas Hometown Hero
Wrangling a Christmas Cowboy
Wrangling a Wild Texan—coming February 2025

Kingman Ranch Series
Charming a Texas Beast
Charming a Knight in Cowboy Boots
Charming a Big Bad Texan
Charming a Fairytale Cowboy
Charming a Texas Prince
Charming a Christmas Texan
Charming a Cowboy King

Bad Boy Ranch Series:
Taming a Texas Bad Boy
Taming a Texas Rebel
Taming a Texas Charmer
Taming a Texas Heartbreaker
Taming a Texas Devil

Taming a Texas Rascal
Taming a Texas Tease
Taming a Texas Christmas Cowboy

Brides of Bliss Texas Series:
Spring Texas Bride
Summer Texas Bride
Autumn Texas Bride
Christmas Texas Bride

Tender Heart Texas Series:
Falling for Tender Heart
Falling Head Over Boots
Falling for a Texas Hellion
Falling for a Cowboy's Smile
Falling for a Christmas Cowboy

Deep in the Heart of Texas Series:
Going Cowboy Crazy
Make Mine a Bad Boy
Catch Me a Cowboy
Trouble in Texas
Flirting with Texas
A Match Made in Texas
The Last Cowboy in Texas
My Big Fat Texas Wedding

Overnight Billionaires Series:
A Billionaire Between the Sheets
A Billionaire After Dark
Waking up with a Billionaire

Hunk for the Holidays Series:
Hunk for the Holidays
Ring in the Holidays
Unwrapped

About the Author

KATIE LANE IS a firm believer that love conquers all and laughter is the best medicine. Which is why you'll find plenty of humor and happily-ever-afters in her contemporary and western contemporary romance novels. A USA Today Bestselling Author, she has written numerous series, including *Deep in the Heart of Texas, Hunk for the Holidays, Overnight Billionaires, Tender Heart Texas, The Brides of Bliss Texas, Bad Boy Ranch, Kingman Ranch,* and *Holiday Ranch*. Katie lives in Albuquerque, New Mexico, and when she's not writing, she enjoys reading, eating chocolate (dark, please), and snuggling with her high school sweetheart and cairn terrier, Roo.

For more on her writing life or just to chat, check out Katie here:
FACEBOOK
www.facebook.com/katielaneauthor
INSTAGRAM
www.instagram.com/katielanebooks.

And for more information on upcoming releases and great giveaways, be sure to sign up for her mailing list at www.katielanebooks.com!

Printed in Great Britain
by Amazon